# THE BROKEN HEART

**Unmarriageable**

**Book 4**

# Mary Lancaster

© Copyright 2020 by Mary Lancaster
Text by Mary Lancaster
Cover by Dar Albert

Dragonblade Publishing, Inc. is an imprint of Kathryn Le Veque Novels, Inc.
P.O. Box 7968
La Verne CA 91750
ceo@dragonbladepublishing.com

Produced in the United States of America

First Edition January 2020
Print Edition

Reproduction of any kind except where it pertains to short quotes in relation to advertising or promotion is strictly prohibited.

All Rights Reserved.

The characters and events portrayed in this book are fictitious. Any similarity to real persons, living or dead, is purely coincidental and not intended by the author.

## ARE YOU SIGNED UP FOR DRAGONBLADE'S BLOG?

You'll get the latest news and information on exclusive giveaways, exclusive excerpts, coming releases, sales, free books, cover reveals and more.

Check out our complete list of authors, too!

No spam, no junk. That's a promise!

### Sign Up Here

www.dragonbladepublishing.com

*Dearest Reader;*

*Thank you for your support of a small press. At Dragonblade Publishing, we strive to bring you the highest quality Historical Romance from the some of the best authors in the business. Without your support, there is no 'us', so we sincerely hope you adore these stories and find some new favorite authors along the way.*

*Happy Reading!*

*CEO, Dragonblade Publishing*

# Additional Dragonblade books by Author Mary Lancaster

### Imperial Season Series
Vienna Waltz
Vienna Woods
Vienna Dawn

### Blackhaven Brides Series
The Wicked Baron
The Wicked Lady
The Wicked Rebel
The Wicked Husband
The Wicked Marquis
The Wicked Governess
The Wicked Spy
The Wicked Gypsy
The Wicked Wife
Wicked Christmas (A Novella)
The Wicked Waif
The Wicked Heir
The Wicked Captain
The Wicked Sister

### Unmarriageable Series
The Deserted Heart
The Sinister Heart
The Vulgar Heart
The Broken Heart

**\*\*\* Please visit Dragonblade's website for a full list of books and authors. Sign up for Dragonblade's blog for sneak peeks, interviews, and more: \*\*\***
www.dragonbladepublishing.com

# CHAPTER ONE

I SABELLE DE RENARDE advanced toward the Hart Inn with an odd, nervous dread.

It might have been the ominous darkness of the evening, or the eternally drizzling rain trickling down her carriage window. But more likely, the feeling was rooted in the past.

The last time she had come here, only three months ago, she had been afraid her treacherous husband had shot her one-time lover. As indeed he had, though it had been Pierre, her husband, who had died.

Isabelle had never regretted the fact. Having discovered what he was and what he was doing—betraying the country that had taken him in when his own would have executed him—her last remaining tatters of affection or loyalty had died with him. But that old shame and alarm seemed to be twisting through her stomach now as she approached a far more pleasurable experience: an assignation of love.

In her heart, she hoped he would not have come. That she would spend the night alone, enjoy one of Mrs. Villin's excellent breakfasts in the morning, and then leave, alone. Perhaps she would even call on one of the local landowners …though they would probably not receive the traitor's wife now.

This was not the proper attitude with which to be nearing her tryst. She should be excited, looking forward to a night of intimate bliss. Sir Maurice was a handsome man and his attentions had been balm to her wounded, lonely soul. But at the back of her mind, perhaps she had always known she only considered him because no one else would even speak to her. It wasn't physical love she truly sought from him but human contact. And she liked that he had ignored her husband's notoriety and considered who *she* was, not what Pierre had done.

And yet, the dread remained as the horses slowed, turning into the brightly lit inn yard. She was, deliberately, two hours late. She had tried to tell herself it was so that Sir Maurice wouldn't think her too eager, but in reality, she had been more than half-hoping he would have given up on her and left again.

Even gone to bed would be good.

*No, I should not be here, should I? It is not fair to him or to me. Yet, what else do I have to do to pass the interminable days?*

The carriage door opened. For an instant, she contemplated staying where she was and instructing the coachman to drive back to London through the night. Or even to another inn.

*I have not sunk so low as this…*

But it seemed she had. She could not face another hour of this loneliness. And so, she alighted at the inn's front door.

Stepping into the house's warm glow, Isabelle glanced to the taproom on her right. She glimpsed Sir Maurice Ashton among the revelers, and her stomach lurched painfully.

Elegant and fashionable, he was clearly out of place among the rough fishermen and farmers who made up the bulk of the patrons. Just as clearly, he did not care, but sat aloof and superior, a condescending smile on his lips.

*Drink with them or don't drink with them*, she thought in irritation. *Don't sit among them, despising them and congratulating yourself for not being one of them.*

"Madame de Renarde!" exclaimed Mrs. Villin, the innkeeper's wife, bustling out of the kitchen. "We were not expecting you! Is everything well?"

Hastily, Isabelle stepped forward to avoid being seen from the taproom. Someone else was coming in behind her. "Good evening, Mrs. Villin. Yes, it was a sudden decision, but everything is fine. A bedchamber, if you please, and your private parlor."

"Bless you, madame, the parlor is taken," she said, apparently stricken. "But there's no one in the coffee room this time of night. I can close the door and make sure you're not disturbed."

Isabelle hesitated. Her instinct was to order supper sent up to her bedchamber, simply to avoid Sir Maurice, but that was both unfair and cowardly. Besides, she was very conscious of the people behind her.

"The coffee room is fine," she said, hastening toward it.

But from behind, one of the newcomers was quicker, striding ahead of her and opening the door. "Ma'am."

Impossible to tell his station from that one word, or his undistinguished but respectable dress. But one glance at his wild, dancing dark eyes and she doubted anyone would care. He may have been handsome. She thought he was—bronzed skin, straight nose, generous mouth, enviable cheekbones ... And those amazing eyes, inviting the fun and laughter that was balm to her soul. And yet, behind them, surely, lay a strange desperation...

But she had stared long enough. She allowed him a faint smile as she inclined her head and swept past him into the room. He bowed, perhaps with slight exaggeration, and strode after his friends into the taproom.

"Who is he?" she asked Mrs. Villin as she followed the innkeeper's wife across the room to the fireplace and cast off her traveling cloak and bonnet.

"No idea, madame. Never seen him before in my life. Sit here, where it's warm, and I'll bring you some supper. I have a good mutton soup and a ham and chicken pie."

"Sounds delicious," Isabelle said. This was where she should mention Sir Maurice. *Is Sir Maurice Ashton here, perchance? Please tell him I would be grateful if he would wait on me here in the morning.*

It was his idea. To let him know she had arrived, after which their assignation would be discreet. He had seemed surprised that she was not the one to suggest this subterfuge. But in truth, she was far less wise in the ways of clandestine relationships than he seemed to imagine. She had only ever taken one lover, and he still made her heart ache.

Her tongue stuck to the roof of her mouth. For it came to her that she was still letting Pierre drive her life and her unhappiness. She had gone to Verne for comfort from Pierre's serial adultery. And now she had come to Sir Maurice because of Pierre's treachery. She did not want him. In fact, she'd felt a much stronger tug of attraction to the stranger with the laughing eyes who had bowed her into this room.

She had no excuse for Sir Maurice. And less to dismiss him.

"Is there anything else, madame?" Mrs. Villin asked.

"No," Isabelle said. "Thank you."

"Very good. I'll have your things taken up to your chamber, and Lily will bring your supper directly."

As the woman bustled off, Isabelle sank into the chair nearest the fire and leaned her head back. She had no idea what she would do next, but the very air of the Hart seemed to relax her into something very close to contentment. She felt as though she were still traveling. And if she had not arrived, no decisions were yet necessary.

The door opened a few minutes later to admit Lily, the innkeeper's pretty daughter, who greeted her cheerfully and set the nearest table for her supper. Isabelle could count the number of times she had been here on one hand, but it seemed she was always greeted as a friend. Even now, when the Villins knew the worst of Pierre.

"You are busy tonight," Isabelle observed.

"Yes, the taproom is heaving! But you shouldn't be bothered in here. Are you on your way to Mrs. Longstone's?"

"No," Isabelle replied. Her cousins, the Longstones, had made it clear that although they would not cut her off precisely, she was no longer welcome in their house. Which was undeniably hurtful since she and not Pierre was their blood relation, and since she had acted as governess to Mrs. Longstone's orphaned granddaughter for no more than her board. She missed the child, Jane. She missed being useful.

Lily poured her a glass of wine and brought it to her. "Are you keeping well, madame?"

Isabelle met the girl's gaze in some surprise. "I? Of course."

Just for a moment, Lily's gaze was uncomfortably perceptive, and Isabelle met it with a somewhat childish defiance.

"And how are you, Lily?" she asked amiably. "Has no handsome young farmer managed to persuade you to marriage?"

"No, I am happy where I am! Though I think my father would like me to accept Ned Bunton at Underton Farm."

"Don't you like him?"

"Ned?" She laughed. "Of course I like him. But I have known him all my life. I feel I should marry someone new, not a man I regard as a brother."

"There is a lot to be said for a man you already know. Less unpleasant surprises."

"Is that what happened to you, madame? Unpleasant surprises?"

Isabelle gave her a crooked smile. "You are right, of course. Such surprises are always possible, however long the acquaintance. So, if you will not take the estimable Mr. Bunton, what will you do?"

"Follow my heart, or take no husband at all."

It was a sweet, uncomplicated view of the world. But then, she had a family who loved her, a home, an occupation.

Isabelle raised her glass to the girl. "I wish you every happiness."

Lily smiled dazzlingly and went out. She returned only a few minutes later with bowls and platters of food. Paying for this night would just about use up Isabelle's dwindling supply of money. After this... Right now, she didn't really care.

Thanking Lily, she sat at the table and did justice to Mrs. Villin's excellent cooking.

Only as she finished her apple and cinnamon tart did she become aware of the voices outside her window. It was more of a low hum than distinguishable words, but something about the tone made her think the conversation was in French.

Curiously, she rose from the table, walked to the window, and drew back the curtain.

Three men, deep in conversation, stood between the front door of the inn and the coffee room window. The rain had gone off, and from the clearing sky, moonlight spilled down on them, joining the glow from the lanterns at the front door. The movement of the curtain, or perhaps the extra candlelight from her window, drew their attention. All three turned in her direction, and she saw that one was the man who had opened the coffee room door for her. He said something, low, urgent, and commanding to the others, who immediately trotted off into the night.

On impulse, Isabelle reached up and threw open the window.

"Can I help you, ma'am?" the remaining man called, strolling toward her. He moved with a sort of wary, controlled grace, quite at odds with his untamed, reckless eyes. A man of intriguing contradictions.

"I was about to ask you the same question," Isabelle replied. "You and your friends gave the impression of having lost something."

"Someone," he corrected. "Our friends should have been here some time ago." He came to a halt, his gaze flickering beyond her into the room.

"They have probably lost their way. The Hart is not on the main road, after all."

"It isn't," he agreed. "So, what brings so fine a lady as yourself to such an out of the way establishment?"

"I lived near here for some years."

"Nostalgia is the thief of life," he observed. "One must move forward."

"You are entirely right. Is that why you and your friends are here?"

"Of course. You did not see our other friends on the road?"

"I'm afraid I was a little distracted. I saw no other carriages that I can recall for at least an hour before we arrived."

"They may have been on horseback."

"If they were there, I'm afraid I missed them,"

A man stepped out of the inn door. A youngish man in the uniform of the royal navy. Without warning, Isabelle's companion threw himself over the windowsill and into the coffee room. He landed with surprising lightness, rolled, and jumped to his feet.

In shock, Isabelle had stumbled back. Her companion raised one long finger to his lips as he moved purposefully to the window, reached out, and drew it shut.

"Don't be alarmed," he said without looking at her. Instead, he was peering through the gap in the curtain toward the front door. "I mean you no harm."

"Are you hiding from someone?" she demanded.

"Yes."

She hadn't expected him to admit it quite so freely. "The naval officer?"

He shot a quick grin at her and returned to his observation, "Yes."

"Why?"

"He seems uncommonly curious, not to say disapproving."

Enlightenment dawned. She almost laughed. "Are you a smuggler, sir?"

"Sort of," he admitted, relaxing onto the window seat and adjusting the curtain to watch his quarry with greater ease.

"Do you imagine he will try to arrest you in this place?"

"I'm not sure what he will do. Which is why I watch."

"Do you think you could do it from a different window?" she suggested.

"Of course." He dragged his gaze from the window and stood. "I would hate your husband to call me out over a misunderstanding."

"That would be most alarming," she agreed.

"He's gone back inside anyway. Alone." He walked halfway to the coffee room door before he paused and turned back to her. "You will not give me away?"

"I have no interest in smugglers, sir, and no one would listen to me if I did."

"Not even your husband?" he asked.

"My husband does not listen to anything anymore," she said dryly. "He is dead."

Her visitor started back toward her in sudden contrition. "I'm sorry."

"Don't be," she said at once. "I'm not."

He paused, his head tilted to one side as he regarded her. "Well that is honest. Or is it heartless?"

"Both."

"No."

She blinked. "No?"

"You are not heartless. Not with those eyes."

Shaken, she dragged her gaze free. No, she had never been heartless, but she had spent so long convincing people she was, that the words of this stranger threw her.

"I imagine *your* eyes tell a more interesting story," she accused. "Though I doubt it would be fit for the ears of a lady."

He raised his dark eyebrows. "What makes you think that?"

"Nothing," she admitted. "But I have always found attack to be an excellent defense."

A flash of amusement lit his restless face. "I wish we had time to compare stories. But I fear that is doomed to remain one of my life's regrets."

"Of course, you are in a hurry to return to your smuggling."

8

"Also," he reminded her, "you dismissed me."

"So I did, and yet here you still are."

As though he took her words as a challenge, he walked back toward her. "You distracted me."

"If so, you are too easily distracted."

A breath of laughter shook him as he halted before her. "Not easily enough." His warm, dazzling smile raised sudden butterflies in her stomach, taking her by surprise.

He was tall, forcing Isabelle to look up. "What do you mean by that?"

"It's part of the story we have no time for." Unexpectedly, he took her hand. The touch of his fingers was intense. "Thank you for hiding me from your Royal Navy."

His eyes, those wild, laughing, yet almost desperate eyes, were not those of a rake, a seducer. So why did she feel she was being seduced?

"It is not my navy," she said nervously. "Or my country, in truth."

He blinked. "It isn't?"

Her eyebrows flew up, for although she spoke fluent English, no one had ever accused her of doing so without a trace of a French accent. "I think you are not as observant as you imagine. I am an émigrée."

His gaze held hers. "I suppose I hoped you were not."

"Why?"

His lips curved. "Many reasons." He raised her hand and kissed it, a light, brief caress that stirred every nerve in her body. Then he released her. "Mostly, because you are much too delightful to have anything to do with a man like Maurice Ashton."

Her mouth fell open. By the time she had shut it again, the door was closing softly behind him.

She sank onto the nearest chair, then jumped up, frowning, and began to pace around the room.

What the devil had he meant by that? Was he a friend of Ashton's?

Could Sir Maurice possibly have been blabbing about his assignation? In the public taproom of an inn?

Her face flamed, and she covered it with her fingers in a vain attempt to cool it. It seemed she had made many mistakes in coming here. Only her instinct to stay silent about Sir Maurice in Lily's presence had been correct.

She would leave tomorrow at first light. Though why she should care about her reputation still, she had no idea. Pierre had already made that pointless. No, it wasn't so much her reputation that moved her. It was more outrage that she had been duped. Shame from many sources curled her toes.

She needed to get away from this wretched country. Perhaps she could go to America, if she could only scrape together enough money for her passage. Though, of course, there was war there, too. She felt suddenly trapped in the Hart, in the country, in her whole life as she had made it.

Fortunately, perhaps, Lily came in then to clear away the supper leftovers.

Isabelle watched her for a little in silence. Then she said abruptly. "Lily, have you been in the taproom this evening?"

"Yes, helping Dad out when I can."

"I thought I saw Sir Maurice Ashton there when I arrived."

"Fashionable gent?" Lily asked. "Yes, he's there. Is he a friend of yours?"

*I very much doubt it.* "Merely an acquaintance. Tell me, did you happen to notice if he is with friends?"

"He arrived on his own," Lily recalled. "Well, with his valet and groom, which is about as close to alone as a gentleman gets! He's been sitting with Lieutenant Steel, the navy officer. Well, both gentlemen together, I suppose. And the other strangers—they've been sitting at Sir Maurice's table, too."

"What other strangers?"

"Gentlemen who arrived right about when you did, madame."

"And are they friends of Sir Maurice?"

Lily shrugged. "They may be now. Weren't when they arrived, for I heard them all introducing themselves to each other."

"And who are they?" Isabelle asked curiously. "What are their names?"

Lily thought. "Black. The one who talks most, with the eyes, is Black. Can't remember the others, if I heard them, which I doubt."

*With the eyes.* It could only be her visitor. Mr. Black. "Lily, I wonder if you—"

Before she could finish her sentence, several shouts blasted from the taproom, followed by an almighty crash, such as furniture falling. Lily dropped her tray and as one, she and Isabelle bolted out of the coffee room to see what on earth had happened.

# CHAPTER TWO

C APTAIN ARMAND LE Noir collected distractions like richer men might collect fine porcelain. Which was one reason he kept volunteering for the insanely risky tasks offered by his commanders. By those standards, landing in England at night to meet escaped prisoners of war and return them to France gave him little concern, even when said prisoners failed to turn up outside the inn at the right time.

And so, whiling away the irritating waiting time, his restless mind had plenty of room to be distracted by the beautiful émigrée who had entered the inn just in front of him. She of the tall, elegant figure and the swan-like neck, of the shining golden hair and the haunted, almost desperate eyes. She who had made barely any fuss at all about him catapulting himself into her solitude an hour later. That had intrigued him. And he'd rather liked her understated humor, the lazy laughter lurking behind her brilliant, gray-green eyes. He'd guessed her purpose here, of course, almost as soon as he'd first strolled into the busy taproom, looking about him as any stranger would.

The patrons were largely ordinary country folk and fisherman, though a man of around his own age in the uniform of the Royal Navy did give him a moment's pause. However, he appeared to be sitting alone, with some space between him and the only aristocratic looking gentleman in the room. This was an elegantly-dressed civilian with short brown hair brushed forward over a sharp-nosed, yet somehow soft face.

Letting his gaze merely glide over them, Noir found no sign of the men he sought, no one, indeed, very interested in him or his two companions.

There were other seats available in the room, but with his usual reckless tempting of fate, Noir chose to sit at the table with the naval officer and the aristo. As he did so, he flicked his gaze at his men, advising them it might be best to sit elsewhere. But they ignored him, as they occasionally did, and sat stolidly on either side of him.

"What can I get you, gentlemen?" asked the pretty serving girl.

"Ale, if you please," Noir replied in his best English. "Unless you have a decent brandy?"

The aristocratic Englishman smiled and raised his own amber glass.

"I can bring you both, sir," the girl said cheerfully.

"Have we missed the joke?" Noir asked the aristocrat after agreeing to the girl's suggestion.

But it was the naval officer who answered in a disapproving voice. "Only because the brandy *is* good. It is clearly French and has therefore been smuggled by those in league with the enemy."

"Oh, come, sir," the aristocrat drawled. "There's been smuggling along this coast since duty was invented! You can't accuse the 'gentlemen' of treason."

"I can, and I do," the officer retorted. "I have personally come across such creatures, and they do not care the damage they do. Cut-throat traitors!"

Noir, with good reason not to discuss what was smuggled in and out of England or France, merely accepted his ale and brandy from the girl. He clinked glasses with his friends and murmured to his English companions, "Your health, gentlemen."

The naval officer, perhaps feeling he had been too forceful in his condemnation for a convivial evening, made an effort toward pleasant conversation. He offered Noir his hand. "My name is Steele, lieutenant aboard His Majesty's ship, *Resolute*."

Noir shook hands. "Black. This is Bush and Carter," he added, indicating Boucher and Caron beside him.

When their hands were duly shaken, too, the aristocrat finally offered his hand to Noir. "The name's Ashton. Sir Maurice Ashton."

"How do you do?" Noir murmured politely, and they all shook hands with Ashton, too.

Noir found it amusing to be so quickly accepted by English gentlemen. In fact, he had more than half expected his accent not to pass muster and be forced to fall back on his émigré story. Which was even funnier. That he, the nameless Paris street orphan, should play the great aristocrat who'd fled from the revolution. However, since he had called himself Black, he left the matter alone.

"Are you staying overnight at the inn, gentlemen?" Lieutenant Steele asked.

"No, we mean to ride back to Finsborough," Noir replied with a quick glance toward the door where two locals were leaving. Where the devil *were* the men he was meant to meet? "Is it a comfortable house?"

"Oh, I hope so," Aston said with a lascivious smile. He glanced around his companions with superior amusement. "Between ourselves, I have an assignation."

Noir had less than no interest in the man's affairs.

Even Lieutenant Steele curled his lips with distaste. "I cannot imagine Mrs. Villin will approve of your bringing your doxies here, sir."

The aristocrat laughed. "Doxies? My dear sir, do you really imagine I would have strayed so far out of London for a mere doxy? Oh, no, my bird of paradise is something quite different! In fact, her family far outranks mine. She possesses incomparable beauty, a figure to admire, and a burning desire for your humble servant." He almost purred. "More than that, she is exotic and foreign. French, in fact."

Caron let out a snort which he quickly changed to a sneeze.

Noir thought of the beautiful lady with the haunting eyes for whom he had opened the door, and wondered.

"More smuggling, sir?" he asked wryly.

"You are amusing. Of course, she is an émigrée. From one of the first families in France, as it happens. Her people were lucky to escape. In fact, many of them didn't."

"And so, of course, you take advantage," Steele sneered.

But Sir Maurice Ashton merely smiled. "I have every intention of ensuring the advantage is hers."

Noir sat back, half-amused, half-disbelieving. "Forgive me, but what are you doing here with *us*?"

"She has not yet arrived," Ashton admitted.

*I think perhaps she has...*

"Perhaps she has no intention of coming," Steele taunted.

"Oh, she'll come," Ashton said softly.

Noir found the man's speech contemptible. Boasting of one's conquest of any lady, let alone one of rank, in a public inn, was surely not the behavior of an honorable English gentleman. It was certainly beneath Noir and anyone he had ever called friend.

"You look disapproving, my friend," Ashton drawled, meeting his gaze.

Noir shrugged. "It's none of my business."

He gazed out of the window, willing the four men he awaited to loom out of the darkness. The taproom was emptying as men returned to their families and a good night's sleep before the next day's work. Noir and his men could not linger here much longer without drawing unwanted attention. They would have to wait outside, or go looking...

He rose abruptly, "Excuse me. I believe I need some air. No, I'll be back directly," he added to Boucher and Caron, who clearly meant to follow him. Which would have looked rather ridiculous. He just hoped they would keep their mouths shut or stick to their émigré stories.

Outside was cold, clear, and quiet. It was his own men who loomed out of the darkness to meet him.

"Any sign?" he demanded.

Lefevre shook his head. "We've been walking continuously around the perimeter, but no sign of them."

"Damn them, they should have signaled if something had gone wrong. Either it's *very* wrong or we just have to wait." He scowled at Lefevre. "I'm not good at waiting."

"I know," Lefevre said fervently. "We're all praying they come soon."

Some change in the light, as though someone had opened a curtain or lit a lantern, made him order the men hastily back to their patrolling. While he turned and beheld the beautiful woman he had seen earlier.

*Oh yes, this would be distraction…*

*Leave her alone. She suffers enough if she is indeed that fool's mistress.*

And then she threw the window wide and nothing short of arrest could have kept him from striding toward her…

In the brief, intriguing encounter that followed, he had found himself hoping he was mistaken. That she had nothing to do with Ashton. For despite the confident tilt of her head, and the seductive sophistication of her manner, he sensed some deeper vulnerability in her. And he could discern no French in her accent. But then she admitted she was an émigrée and he was sure.

He might have despised Ashton's boastful remarks, but he could understand the obsession that caused him to make them.

He meant his parting shot. *"You are much too delightful to have anything to do with a man like Maurice Ashton."*

Returning to the taproom with his mind too full of this heady new distraction, he found his men still awkwardly drinking their ale while Steele and Ashton bickered. His men sat up, looking openly relieved when he walked in.

"Ah," Steele said. "I took some air myself, but I didn't see you."

"No? I strolled around a bit." Noir resumed his seat, lifted the remains of his brandy, and smiled.

But for some reason, the suspicious Steele's eyes had narrowed. "Is that a hint of French I hear in your accent?" he asked abruptly.

For once, Noir cursed his distraction. "It could be," he admitted brazenly. "Perhaps I have not yet lost it all."

"You, too, are an émigré?" Ashton said in surprise. "Called Black?"

"Le Noir. I anglified it." He allowed himself a wintry smile. "We émigrés are not all aristocrats."

"Even so," Ashton said. "You must be an acquaintance of the Renardes."

Lieutenant Steele was looking suspicious again.

For some reason, Noir felt his answer to Ashton's question should be *yes*. But there were far too many pitfalls to claiming acquaintance with people he'd never heard of. He'd had enough of this work, wanted merely to recover his Frenchmen and go. He'd rather fight his way off the beach than sit here lying like some damned spy.

"No," he said baldly.

The Englishmen wore almost identical expressions of civil disbelief. "It's funny how few people know Renarde now," Ashton observed. "Once, he was such a popular man."

"Acquit me," Noir said impatiently. "I've never even heard of him. What is your—"

"Never heard of him?" Steele interrupted, staring at him. "The dead traitor who has the entire émigré population fighting to prove its loyalty?"

"It seems we moved in different circles," Noir said impatiently. "Do you accuse me of some crime in not knowing your dead traitor?"

"Hardly," Ashton said peaceably. "It's simply surprising."

But Steele, it seemed, was like a terrier with a rat. "Where did you say you were staying in Finsborough?"

"I didn't," Noir said gently.

Abruptly, Steele switched his hard gaze to Caron. "Then which is your favorite inn in the town? The George or the Dragon?"

Frowning, Caron had clearly been following the conversation with some difficulty. "Dragon," he said randomly.

Mentally, Noir cast his eyes to heaven. And laughed, which seemed to throw the Englishmen, though only for an instant.

"There is no inn called the Dragon in Finsborough," Steele said triumphantly. "Sirs, I take leave to tell you that I doubt very much you are who you pretend!"

"Well," Noir said, rising to his feet. "Since we are clearly no longer welcome, we shall take our leave."

Obediently, his men rose with him. Ashton sat back, waiting to be entertained. But Lieutenant Steele jumped up and did the one thing guaranteed to cause disaster to all.

He drew his sword.

It had been hanging discreetly at his side all the time, almost part of him. And the screech of it leaving its sheath attracted the attention of everyone left in the taproom.

"Don't," Noir said to his men, but it was too late. They were already drawing their own weapons in defense of their captain.

"Here!" the innkeeper bellowed, though with more resignation than alarm or even much surprise. "None of that! Outside, now, before I call the—"

The rest of his words were lost as Steele upended the table, forcing the Frenchmen to fall backward. He leapt agilely over the table with the clear intent of disarming and capturing all three of them. There might have been enough people in the taproom to help him do, it, too. Though not without a blood bath.

"Caron, get everyone back to the far side," Noir barked in French. "Boucher, the front door. No one else comes in and no one leaves."

# CHAPTER THREE

IN THE HALLWAY, a man dashed past Isabelle and Lily to the front door. But he wasn't running away. He shot the bolts, then turned his back to the door. Grim-faced, he drew his pistol.

Lily emitted a squeak of outrage.

"Put that away, imbecile!" Isabelle commanded and strode purposefully across the hall without waiting to see if he would obey her. Often, she had discovered, the assumption she would be obeyed was enough to make it happen. She prayed it would here, because she certainly had no means to compel him.

Inside the taproom was chaos. A duel appeared to be taking place.

Isabelle's recent visitor, Mr. Black, and the naval officer—Lieutenant Steele?—were fighting with swords across fallen tables and chairs, while another man, also armed with a pistol, had herded the handful of other drinkers to the far end of the room, along with Mr. and Mrs. Villin. And Sir Maurice who stood slightly apart, with his held high and his lip curled with distaste.

Outraged, Isabelle started toward the fighters, but the armed man from the front door had followed them and commanded, "No! Do not go in."

Lily clutched Isabelle's arm, though whether to prevent Isabelle from moving or to try and hold herself back, wasn't clear.

"You're French," Isabelle said blankly to the gunman, thinking aloud without even looking at him. Instead, her attention was fixed on the duelists in the taproom.

In the early days of her marriage, Isabelle had watched a fencing demonstration, a fascinating dance of agility and speed performed with courtesy and panache—and buttoned foils so that no one got hurt. This fight was nothing like that. For one thing, they did not use rapiers but swords that seemed, like their owners, to have fought in many a battle before this. It was rough and brutal, and Steele's face both grim and desperate.

Black, on the other hand, seemed actually to be smiling. She even heard him laugh, breathless but definite. His wild eyes shone with fierce enjoyment. His every move seemed imbued with something very like relief.

And then, as he spun around, he caught sight of Isabelle in the doorway. For the tiniest instant, his gaze held hers, and that moment of inattention was enough for Steele to break through his guard. Black managed a last moment partial deflection, but Steele's sword still slashed through his sleeve.

In suddenly refocused fury, Black drove his opponent back and back, giving him no opening, no defense but retreat until he stumbled over the fallen table. With a sudden twist of the wrist, Black's sword wrenched Steele's free, sent it flying and tumbling to the floor. His weapon followed through inexorably, sliding into his foe's shoulder.

Steele cried out, his knees buckling. Oddly, it was Black who caught him in his free arm and dragged him across to the nearest intact bench where he let him slump.

Black whirled around. His sword swept through the air, along the huddle of appalled people at the back of the room, until it pointed straight at Mrs. Villin.

"You. Look after him, if you please."

Mrs. Villin, after a quick glance at her husband, edged past Black toward the wounded officer. Distractedly, Black wiped his sword against his coat and slid it back into the scabbard that had clearly been hidden beneath, even when he'd thrown himself through the coffee room window. When he dragged his sleeve across his sweaty brow, he left blood behind, but he didn't seem to notice.

Only then did he really regard the alarmed but outraged Englishmen huddled together, glaring at him in indignation for daring to defeat their champion. He laughed.

"*I* should have fought you!" Sir Maurice Ashton said with a mixture of grandeur and bitterness.

"One day, maybe." Black didn't appear to be listening. Instead, his frowning gaze was on Isabelle and Lily who had crept into the room unnoticed.

Isabelle decided to take charge.

Shaking Lily off, she swept into the middle of the room, drawing all eyes. "What in God's name is going on here? None of you should be armed in this place!" She halted in front of Black, glaring at him and holding out her hands. "Give me your weapons. Now."

Vaguely, she was aware of the reactions around her. At least one of Black's allies grinned. Sir Maurice's mouth fell open. Several eyed her with alarm. But she let neither her gaze nor her arms waver.

Black seemed almost stunned. Then an appreciative gleam lightened his eyes. It might even have been admiration.

"I am almost tempted to obey, madame. Be so good as to sit." He took one of her outstretched hands and tugged her unexpectedly toward a chair which she almost fell into.

He turned to the door where one of his armed allies had reappeared. "Anyone else?"

The man shook his head and only when he replied in French, did she realize Black had addressed him in the same language. "No. I locked the back door from the kitchen."

"Hmm." Black frowned, then sighed. "Very well. Boucher, you and Caron, fetch everyone out of the bedchambers and bring them to the coffee room across the hall. In fact, let us *all* repair to the coffee room, so we need not guard both places." He regarded Isabelle with a quirk of his expressive lips. "I'm afraid your solitude is over, madame."

NOIR HAD A problem. Several problems. A wounded naval officer who might die and a collection of resentful captives whom he couldn't release in case word of his presence got out with them. And no escaped prisoners to take back to France. And the boat would not wait for him forever.

Having poked around the other ground floor rooms, he found an empty parlor—hired by Ashton who had, presumably hoped for a cozier evening with his lover. While his men extracted the guests from their bedchambers, he took another walk around the grounds of the inn, hoping for any sign of the men he had come for. He walked as far as the road, even knelt down with his ear literally on the ground in the hope of hearing horses' hooves, but there was nothing.

Wiping off his ear and his clothes, he strode back to the inn. The slash in his arm was hurting, and he knew he should deal with it. However, a new thought struck him. The innkeeper had been angry about the fight, but he hadn't been surprised. And if Noir and his companions had been recognized as French, wasn't it perfectly possible that the escaped prisoners-of-war had also been recognized? The innkeeper could be holding them, hiding them until the authorities came.

Which would be another *huge* problem.

He marched back into the inn by the back door and locked it with one of the keys extracted from the innkeeper and his wife, then continued through the kitchen and the hall into the coffee room— where he found another problem.

"A child!" he groaned, staring at the boy of about three years old asleep on his mother's lap. "Why would anyone bring a child to this benighted place?"

"Presumably his parents had not heard it would be overrun by French cutthroats," his beautiful émigrée said with sarcasm.

Noir scowled, which seemed to terrify the child's mother and seriously alarm the spectacled man beside them, who might have been a schoolteacher or a clergyman. So, he hastily transferred his attention to the émigrée.

It annoyed him further to see she sat beside her lover, the pair of them looking as elegant and sophisticated as though attending a royal ball instead of being herded at gunpoint in the coffee room of an isolated inn with the common unwashed. On her other side sat the pale figure of Lieutenant Steele, glaring at him with acute dislike.

"Not dead yet, my friend?" Noir said cheerfully. "Excellent."

Steele blinked.

"Since none of us are dead yet," the lady said, "let us keep it that way while we can. Lieutenant Steele needs a physician. Your friends are not here, so you should go before our soldiers arrive."

"Our soldiers," he mocked.

To his surprise, she flushed slightly, though her chin tilted. "I have lived here since I was three years old, monsieur. It is the only home I know. Lieutenant Steele here would like you to stay and be killed or taken. I, being less patient, would advise you to flee before what you fear actually happens."

"And what is it I fear?" he asked with interest.

"Discovery," she shot back. "Why else fight with swords rather than simply shoot your enemy? Why lock the doors and windows and keep us here except to prevent the news of your presence spreading? You're afraid this is a trap, aren't you? You're probably right." She gave him a wintry smile. "I don't believe spies are treated with the same courtesy as military officers."

He curled his lip at her, but he couldn't deny to himself that her words hurt.

"He's no spy," Steele said unexpectedly. "He's a soldier, and he fights like one. His men call him captain. Captain le Noir, I believe."

Noir regarded him thoughtfully. "And the lady?"

"I have not been introduced to the lady."

Again, the lady's chin came up. Her gaze met his with unnecessary defiance. "Isabelle de Renarde."

Renarde. The name with which Steele and Ashton had caught him out. She was the traitor's widow.

No wonder she was vulnerable and lonely enough to consider Maurice Ashton.

He spun away from them, irritated for once by the distraction. He needed to concentrate on the task. Pacing across the room, he drew all eyes. Everyone regarded him in dubious silence.

He halted abruptly. "We came to meet some friends of ours. I would like to know if they have called in here." His roving gaze fell on Villin, the innkeeper, and his lips quirked. "French émigrés, like ourselves."

"Madame de Renarde is the only émigré I've seen here in weeks," Villin said.

"Let us just say foreigners, then."

"Only yourselves."

The Frenchman transferred his thoughtful gaze to Mrs. Villin and Lily. "Perhaps you see more? Or differently?"

"No," said Mrs. Villin uncompromisingly.

"Yet none of you seemed very shocked when the lieutenant challenged me. You were not, I think, surprised by our presence."

"We're not surprised by much," Villin growled.

"No, I can see that. But I smell a trap, Monsieur—Villin, is it?"

"Villin it is, and if you feel trapped, please make use of the front door!"

"Nothing would give me more pleasure. But I need my friends."

"They're not here."

He frowned at the Villins for a few more moments. "I don't believe you," he said at last. "And yet there are no soldiers battering at your door to take us captive. I think we came too early for you. I think you have my friends hidden, and the soldiers have not yet got here."

"If that's what you believe, you should run while you can," Villin retorted.

Noir swept up the vacant chair from Madame de Renarde's table and sat facing the innkeeper. "Where do you keep your smuggled brandy?"

Villin blinked. "Nothing smuggled here," he said self-righteously. "Everything pays proper duty."

"Liar. But you must have a secret room, a cellar, perhaps, to hide it from excisemen."

"Never had trouble with such," Villin maintained.

"Why? Do you bribe them?" Noir asked wryly, though he did not expect an answer and got none. "Look, I *know* you have a hidden store. I don't *actually* know if the foreign gentlemen made it here, but I *think* they did. Since there are no soldiers waiting for us, I can only assume they are still here. You see my reasoning?"

Villin scratched his head. "I see it. But I don't understand it."

"It's flawed," Madame de Renarde pointed out.

Noir transferred his gaze to her. If she feared him, there was no sign of it in her brilliant, haunted eyes. More likely, she despised him.

She said, "You have no evidence your friends were here. You only think they *should* be because, presumably, of some communication that must be days old. Lots of things could have happened in that time. You only *want* Villin to have hidden them because that would make your life simpler."

"Izzy, Izzy," Sir Maurice murmured beside her. "Don't antagonize the...gentleman."

"I'm not a gentleman," Noir snapped, stupidly annoyed by the Englishman's familiarity with her. "Therefore, I have no hesitation in asking this lady if she suspects where I should look for my friends."

"How could I possibly know that?" she countered. She considered. "Which direction were they coming from?"

"I don't believe I need a road guide. Mr. Villin." He swung suddenly back to the innkeeper. "Here is what will happen. Either you show me your secret room, whether or not it contains my friends, or my men and I shall look for it ourselves. We will not be as gentle as you."

Villin stared back at him. Mrs. Villin and Lily exchanged glances, then lowered their eyes. No one spoke.

The Frenchman shrugged. "Very well. Boucher. You and Lefevre go down the cellar stairs from the kitchen and start looking. Investigate the walls and the floor, if necessary. You needn't be too careful of the bottles and barrels that get in your way. Speed is of the essence. I'll join you shortly."

He stood and walked out of the room. Purposefully, he crossed the hall and entered the empty taproom. There, he peeled off his coat and examined his wound with some annoyance. It really needed a stitch or two, or at least a good clean to get the fluff from his shirt out of it. However, he had no time for that. It no longer bled much, so he simply tore both the sleeves off his shirt. The right sleeve took a heroic effort and a lot of grimacing, since it made the wound hurt like the devil. However, he made a pad out of the bloody one and tied it on with the clean one. He was just pulling the knot tight with his teeth when Isabelle de Renarde walked in.

He scowled at her. "How did you get in here?"

"I walked. Since you locked all the doors and windows and we can't get out, there is really no point in forcing us all to stay in one place. Don't worry—your man threatened me most ferociously."

"Not ferociously enough, apparently."

"Well, I told him I was going to attend to your wound."

"Why?" he asked in surprise. "You have something to tell me?"

She stared. "No. I just told you. I've come to attend to your wound."

"A mere scratch," he said suspiciously. "And already tended. Though I thank you for your...surprising care."

"So you should," she agreed, walking behind the counter and returning with a jug of water and the medicine box Mrs. Villin had already used on Lieutenant Steele. "Sit," she commanded.

When he stayed where he was, she merely walked up to him and began untying the rough bandage he had just applied. Her shining, gold hair smelled of summer flowers. The touch of her fingers was light and deft, and so he merely watched her, letting her work. She could, he supposed, overcome him by tearing savagely at his wound. Or stabbing him with those vicious little scissors in the medicine box. Curiously, he waited to see if she would.

She only drew in her breath at the sight of the gory injury. Surrounded by dried blood which had trickled down his arm, it looked worse than it was. He hoped.

"Hold out your arm," she instructed.

Still curious, he obeyed, watching with faint amusement as she poured water from the jug over the wound, sluicing out all the linen threads and fluff. With a soft cloth from the box, she dried up around the gaping edges. He couldn't deny that it looked better, so he said nothing.

She was rummaging in the box.

"What now?" he asked. "Are you not going to bind up my wounds once more?"

"Not until I have applied something to prevent infection."

"Use the brandy," he advised. "It's quickest. And most effective."

"It will hurt."

"I'm aware."

"Is that why you didn't use it yourself?"

"No, I couldn't be bothered with the fuss." He walked over to the counter, found the brandy bottle, and brought it back. He could have poured the brandy over the hurt himself. But he chose to hand her the bottle and watch her face as, after a quick, apologetic glance at him, she splashed brandy over the wound.

His flesh cringed with the pain. His breath hissed. But he fixed his gaze on her face and didn't move. He could feel the warmth of her so close to him, the gentle touch of her fingers as she wrapped an entirely different bandage around his arm.

"I ruined my best shirt for nothing," he observed.

"Sew the sleeves back on," she challenged.

"Don't think I won't. Aren't you afraid they'll think you a traitor?"

"They already think I'm a traitor," she said sardonically. "Tarred, as it were, by my late husband's brush."

"Then why do you risk helping me? Why are you here?"

She let her hands fall from his arm, and he missed them. But she didn't yet stand back, simply raised her gaze to his face. "To ask you again to go. I don't believe your friends are here. The Villins are used to strange goings-on in their house. That is why you don't see the depth of surprise you think you should."

"Perhaps."

She frowned. "You are stubborn. And wrong."

"Who knows? I may be stubborn and right. Thank you for your ministrations. You will now return to the coffee room, and I shall join the search in the cellar. Unless you wish to join me there?"

"No, I would rather wait up here while you bury yourself in falling masonry, and when the British soldiers come, I shall show them your bodies."

"Oh, ye of little faith," he said flippantly.

For a moment, neither of them moved, as though that might be construed as a sign of giving in. In reality, Noir enjoyed standing so close to her. She was tall for a woman, and he wouldn't have to lower his head very far to—

He blinked and stepped aside, inviting her to go before him. She went, unhurriedly and with her head held high.

# CHAPTER FOUR

FOR SOME REASON, the encounter with Captain le Noir left Isabelle shaken. Concentrating on tending his wound had been hard enough, feeling his intense gaze on her face the whole time she worked. But when she'd finally raised her gaze to his… He did not have easy eyes to withstand. Hard, yet intense. Giving nothing away. Which didn't mean there was nothing there. He looked too much at her, *saw* too much.

But it was more than his eyes, more even than the handsome face they were set in. Standing close to him…disturbed her. He was the enemy, a dangerous, unpredictable enemy.

When she returned to the coffee room, he left her at the door— after glaring at the guard who had failed to prevent her leaving. The soldier—she presumed they were all soldiers—merely shrugged apologetically without noticeable alarm. They all knew that Isabelle walking from one room to another made no difference to anything. The doors were locked, and she could not have got out without a couple of strong men and a battering ram.

Sir Maurice stood as she entered, clearly waiting to hand her into the vacant chair she had occupied before. Some thudding in the rooms above made her wince. Hammering began below.

On impulse, she changed direction, swerving toward the Villins instead, and sat down. "They may tear your inn apart," she said abruptly. "Would it not be better simply to show them your secret cellar?"

"No." Villin grinned. "Looking will keep them busy."

"Until what?" She gazed at him, wondering if the Frenchman was right about traps.

"Morning, if nothing else, when the alarm's bound to be raised."

Isabelle looked around the few drinkers who had been herded in from the taproom. "Won't they be missed? Will their wives not come looking for them?"

"In the dark? With little ones at home? Not Tapper's missus, nor Johnny's. Reg lives alone. Wouldn't be the first time Bain and Harry had stayed out all night, either. Several times I've swept them out of the taproom the next morning."

"Well, don't tell *them* that," Isabelle warned, nodding her head toward the guard. "We've more chance of being rid of them if they're afraid of discovery."

"They don't seem to be afraid of much," Villin said in disgust. "Swanning in here bold as brass!"

Isabelle lowered her voice further. "If you have a means of signaling anyone who could help—"

"Not from here, madame," Villin said regretfully. "Need to get out onto the marsh."

Isabelle frowned. "We *need* to get out. This is ridiculous."

Villin nodded sympathetically.

His wife leaned forward. "Don't fret, madame," she murmured, and as Isabelle moved closer, she glanced significantly down at her apron. Isabelle's eyes followed instinctively. Mrs. Villin's plump fingers drew a large key partially out of the pocket, then shoved it back in again.

Isabelle smiled at her. "How clever of you."

"Move aside, madame, if you please," the guard interrupted.

Clearly, she was blocking Villin from his view. Like most men, he believed the only danger would come from members of his own sex.

She frowned at him. "My good man, this is silly! The doors are locked. On top of which you have men enough to guard them. Why should we all sit in here?" She pointed to the family at the next table. "This lady and gentleman should at least be allowed to take their child to bed. You cannot frighten him like this!"

The child in question was, in fact, sleeping blissfully through the crashing from above and below and seemed quite oblivious of either angry voices or his parents' tension.

But, rather to Isabelle's surprise, the guard began to look harassed. "Take it up with the captain, madame, not me."

"I will," Isabelle retorted.

But his attitude was interesting. He didn't like holding the family at gunpoint. He was a soldier used to fighting other soldiers, not women and children. If they all felt the same way—and she had a feeling even their captain did, for he hadn't been pleased to see the little boy—then surely it was to the captives' advantage.

Sir Maurice, re-seated once more, was pretending to be asleep when she walked past him. His head rested against the wall behind him, and his eyes were closed. But there was something petulant about his rigidity she did not like. Ignoring him, she continued to the family, whose name she had discovered was Ferris, and sat down beside the mother, being careful not to squash the sleeping child.

"How fortunate he sleeps so soundly," she murmured. "Would you like me to take him for a little to let you rest? I have been a governess, you know."

Mrs. Ferris placed her arm more protectively over the boy.

Isabelle noticed the gesture but persevered. "He would still see you as soon as he wakes."

Mrs. Ferris, looking like a startled deer, said nothing. It was her husband who replied a little hastily. "Thank you, you're very kind, but the movement might wake him."

"Of course." Isabelle hesitated. "I also wanted to say, I do not believe they will hurt him or you, Mrs. Ferris."

"You would say that," Mrs. Ferris burst out. "Being one of them!"

"Marian," her husband protested.

"Well, it's true," Mrs. Ferris insisted, her voice rising with her indignation, loud enough now to attract the attention of the captives as well as the guard. "Don't you see her making up to them as if they are best friends? Of course, because they *are*!"

It was hardly the first accusation of treachery made against her. She said only, "I see no reason why you would imagine so."

"You speak French," Mrs. Ferris muttered.

"I imagine you might, too," Isabelle said wryly. "And your husband almost certainly does."

"She is just overwrought," Mr. Ferris said quickly. "She means nothing by it."

She quite clearly did, but Isabelle let it go. "I only wanted to give you my opinion," she told them, "in case you find it reassuring. I don't believe they are naturally brutal men."

"Tell that to Lieutenant Steele," Mrs. Ferris snapped.

But Isabelle had had enough and rose to her feet. "My dear lady, from what I observed, the lieutenant could easily be dead long since if that was what they wished. So could the rest of us. But if you prefer to wallow in unnecessary fear and alarm for the rest of the night, I shall do nothing to stand in your way."

"I'm sorry ma'am," Ferris said nervously. He lowered his voice. "I do value your opinion, but I doubt it means we can simply walk out the door without being shot."

"Not yet," she agreed. "Excuse me."

"Why do you bother?" Sir Maurice asked as she took the chair opposite him. He didn't trouble to open his eyes.

"Because I know what it is to be afraid," she said. "And I wish it on no one."

His eyes opened. "*Ma chérie*, you have never been afraid of anyone in your life."

She smiled lazily. It had always been what she had wanted people to think. She didn't know why she had admitted to the weakness now, before him of all people, but she was happy enough to go along with his idea that she was joking.

He sat up straighter, smiling back. "It is not quite the escape we planned, is it?"

Although he spoke softly, it was still loud enough for Lieutenant Steele and probably Mr. and Mrs. Ferris to hear, too. Obviously, he saw no need to preserve her reputation—whatever remained of it.

"Not for any of us," she agreed without looking at him. "Lieutenant, how are you?"

"Not much use in a fight, I'm afraid," Steele replied ruefully. He looked very pale and tight-lipped. Clearly, he was in some pain.

"Would a glass of brandy help?" she asked.

"Oh, yes."

"Monsieur," she addressed the guard at once. "May we have a glass of brandy for the lieutenant?"

Mr. Villin stood. "I can get that. In fact, why don't I get refreshments for everyone? My wife could make tea for the ladies." He smiled faintly. "And yourselves."

If there was an insult in his last words, the guard didn't see it. "One at a time," he said. "First, you get brandy for him."

Carefully, Isabelle did not look at Mrs. Villin who no doubt planned to use her key at the first available opportunity. Perhaps she had passed it to her husband. Isabelle's heart began to beat faster as Villin slouched out of the room. But the guard followed him as far as the doorway, from where he could see part of the taproom as well as keep his eye on the rest of his captives.

Villin returned smartly with a large glass of brandy, which he presented to the lieutenant with a bow.

Steele gave him a weary smile in return and reached for the glass with his good arm. "My thanks."

"You might have brought the bottle," Sir Maurice drawled.

"He said one at a time," Villin pointed out, glancing at the guard for permission.

"Sit down," the guard growled. "No one needs more brandy."

"What about tea?" Mrs. Villin asked.

At that moment, quick footsteps in the hall heralded the return of Captain le Noir. There were grimy fingerprints on his face, as though he'd clasped it with his dirty hands. His clothes were no better.

"Tea," he agreed unexpectedly. "Excellent notion. Madame, if you please—for all of us."

Mrs. Villin and Lily both rose to their feet.

"Can't carry all that myself," Mrs. Villin pointed out before either Frenchman could object. "Of course, you're welcome to help if you want, but Lily will be more use."

Captain Noir looked amused. "Undoubtedly," he agreed. "Caron, go with them."

Obediently, their guard, Caron, followed them out of the room while the captain sank into his vacant chair and ran his gaze around all the captives. He didn't linger on Isabelle but on Steele, with his brandy, before moving on. If he had a pistol, he didn't trouble to bring it out. Yet, for some reason, no one took advantage. No one even moved.

"Did you find your missing friends?" Isabelle inquired with undisguised mockery.

He met her gaze. "You know I did not. *Yet.*"

"If you bring down the inn, people might notice."

"I shall, of course, endeavor not to do so."

"You do know you're achieving nothing here," Sir Maurice offered.

"I know I have achieved nothing *yet*," Noir corrected. "The night is young."

"The night is getting on a bit," Sir Maurice retorted. "It's my belief you are not quite sane."

"Then you share the opinion of a good portion of the French army."

"Is that why you are not with the grand army in Russia?" Sir Maurice sneered.

"Oh, no. I'm sure insanity was preferred for that undertaking. Sadly, I was injured and kept back for other tasks."

"Like looking for nonexistent, escaped prisoners?"

"Precisely," Noir agreed.

"But what will happen in Russia?" Isabelle asked. "The Tsar has not surrendered."

"Why should he? He just needs to wait for winter."

"Then the French will retreat?"

"You would have to ask the emperor."

"Then you think he was wrong to invade Russia?" Maurice pounced, openly mocking.

"Of course I do," Noir said unexpectedly. "Utter foolishness and an inevitable waste of life."

Isabelle was intrigued. Sir Maurice, after a stunned moment, said, "Are you not afraid to disagree so openly with your emperor? To criticize him?"

Noir laughed. "Why, are you going to tell him?"

"No, but *she* might," Mrs. Ferris muttered audibly with a glance of loathing at Isabelle. "But, of course, you know who she is and who her husband was."

Noir looked mystified.

"The man you had never heard of," Sir Maurice said helpfully.

Noir's gaze moved quickly from Maurice to Isabelle, and she saw that he already knew.

"What a coincidence," he murmured without interest.

His eyes were unreadable, but again, she thought they saw too much. For example, that Sir Maurice was too busy being clever to stand up for her. For a moment, she even wondered if Noir might defend her himself—which was the one thing guaranteed to make her position worse. But his gaze moved to the door where Mrs. Villin and Lily were entering with trays of cups and tea pots.

"Tea, thank God. I'm parched," Isabelle announced.

Mrs. Villin poured, and Lily carried the first cup and saucer to Noir, who frowned and jerked his head across the room.

Obligingly, Lily brought it to Isabelle. "Go ahead, madame," Lily breathed. "It's not poisoned."

Noir and Caron took theirs last. Then Noir sent his henchman down to help in the cellar. Isabelle thought the soldiers were all down there, now, for she no longer heard bumping from the rooms above.

Sir Maurice, presumably, deduced the same. "I think you might permit us to retire," he said to Noir. "The doors are locked, and you may as easily guard them as all of us. I see no reason why the ladies at least—and the gentlemen among us—should not sleep in as much comfort as is possible in the circumstances. Without inconveniencing you, of course."

"Of course," Noir repeated. "But no. On the whole, I prefer you where I can see you."

"Consider the child," Isabelle pleaded.

He wrenched his gaze free and leapt up. "I said no," he snapped and began pacing the room. Isabelle thought it was so he didn't have to look at the sleeping boy.

Apart from the rhythmic pacing and the odd muffled curse and crash from below, silence fell in the coffee room. In time, all the captives began to nod off.

Isabelle leaned her head back and closed her eyes, too aware of the man moving about the room to sleep. A foot brushed her ankle, which she ignored until a leg pressed against hers. Sir Maurice.

As though shifting in sleep, she turned in her chair, moving her body as far away from him as she could get.

Had she ever enjoyed such blatant flirtation? Yes, once, when she was young, when Pierre had broken her heart, and she had turned to Patrick Verne…

*I loved Patrick. What on earth was I thinking of to come here to a man I don't even like?*

She wondered with odd detachment if she still loved Patrick, who had only ever "nearly" loved her. And who had married a younger and much more lovable woman. A woman who would have been her friend if not for Patrick. But no, his marriage to Cecily seemed to have dampened her own feelings. They were, latterly, only a crutch to hang on to, to prove she could still love. Her heart felt cold and lonely. But a liaison with Maurice Ashton was not the cure for that. She could never love him. He left her…unmoved.

All men did now.

Without warning, the dark, turbulent face of Captain le Noir flitted into her mind. Those wild, desperate eyes and the almost insane stubbornness that drove him. She could not help wondering what his life had been like, what tragedy he hid…

*Oh, yes, typical Isabelle*, she thought ruefully. The only man who had intrigued her in years was a Bonapartist soldier who had taken her prisoner.

With his expressive face dancing across her mind, she drifted into a strange, half-sleeping doze, from which she woke abruptly when someone brushed against her skirts.

*Damn you, Ashton*, she thought in outrage as her eyes snapped open. There was still a lamp lit close by, and by its glow, she saw at once that it had been a much smaller figure than Maurice Ashton who had bumped into her. A small, tousled, blond boy toddled across the room toward the window, while his parents slept, slumped together on the bench.

At the window, Noir appeared to have stopped his relentless pacing to gaze out into the darkness, totally ignoring his captives.

"Hello," the little boy said, arriving beside him.

Noir glanced down at him without obvious surprise. "Good evening."

"Is it still night time? It must be if everyone's asleep."

"I suppose it must."

"You're not asleep," the boy observed.

"That's true.

"What are you looking at?" The boy climbed unaided on to the window seat to peer through the gap in the curtains. "Are you looking for something?"

"Yes, I am, but they aren't there."

"Will you go and look for them in the morning?"

"I don't think I'll be able to."

"I could come with you," the child offered.

Noir's face softened into a smile that made Isabelle's heart beat faster. "I wish you could."

"I'm Sam," the boy said, smiling back and holding up his hand.

"Armand," said Captain le Noir as he bent and solemnly shook the boy's hand.

"What are you doing?" Mrs. Ferris cried, her frightened voice tearing into the rather touching scene. "Get away from him!"

Fortunately, perhaps, the boy dropped Noir's hand to skip across the room to his mother. "Mama, mama, this is my new friend, and please, in the morning, can I help him find his lost things?"

She clutched him to her, ignoring his uncomfortable wriggling. By then, everyone was awake again.

"Take the boy and go to your chamber," le Noir commanded, then glared as the parents simply stared at him. "Quickly, before I change my mind." He resumed his pacing as the family scuttled out of the room.

Little Sam kept trying to look back over his shoulder. "Good night! Good night, Armon!"

"I take it the rest of us are not to be allowed the same courtesy?" Sir Maurice drawled.

"For once, you are entirely correct." Noir stopped at the door, stuck his head out, and yelled out, "Boucher!"

A muffled voice answered from the depths of the building, and Noir strode across the room once more. Another of his men, presumably Monsieur Boucher, trudged wearily in a few moments later, speaking in colloquial French.

"No trace, sir. I don't know where else to look. The bedchambers are clear. There's no easy way into another cellar, and they can't block it up and tear it down every time they get a delivery or want a fresh barrel!"

"I'll take another look," Noir muttered. "You stay here and watch them. Do *not* fall asleep."

"How much longer are we going to wait, Captain?" It was said with resignation, but absolutely no fear.

"I don't know," Noir's voice replied impatiently. He was long out of sight.

Boucher sighed and took out his pistol as he walked across to the window seat, where he sat down and regarded his captives. "Long night," he observed in English.

No one answered him.

Isabelle, aware suddenly of intense observation, turned her head to find Mrs. Villin's gaze upon her. The innkeeper's wife lifted her brows encouragingly and glanced at Boucher.

Isabelle's breath caught. She understood at once that with Noir out of the way and Boucher clearly exhausted, the Villins wanted to take the chance of escape. She could not disagree.

Accordingly, she said, "It must be longer for you, monsieur." And rising, she walked across the room to distract him.

# CHAPTER FIVE

NOIR FOUND LITTLE progress in the cellar. Judging by the length of the place, there was still space unaccounted for beneath the main house. There was just no way into it, not from here or from anywhere else in the inn. No other stairs leading down, and he'd opened every damned cupboard to check, tapped all over every wall in the building.

"Captain, we should be gone," Lefevre said wearily as Noir weaved through the barrels and crates which had been hauled away from the walls. "If you're right and the innkeeper has summoned the soldiers, they could be on us any minute."

Noir kicked the nearest barrel, glowering. "Yes, but if I'm right, then our men are still here. We can't leave them."

"If they're here," Caron said, throwing his pick on the cellar floor, "why don't they answer us when we call? Why don't we hear them?"

"I don't know," Noir said moodily. "Perhaps they don't hear *us*. Damnation, I know they're here." He scowled at his men. "One more hour, and then we must admit defeat. The alternative would be giving the British extra prisoners, namely ourselves." None of them would thrive in a prison. He himself would go insane without distraction. But he *knew* the prisoners were here.

He was aware his men thought he was being unreasonably stubborn. If they weren't men he knew, men he had brought safely out of several other scrapes, they might have defied him and mutinied. But he hadn't forgotten his duty to them.

"Keep looking. I'm going to check the kitchen floor again. We've been ignoring it since it has the entrance to this cellar, but there could be another trapdoor, a secret room below the floor." He hurried back to the stairs, adding over his shoulder, "But you're right about our time here running out. I'll make sure it's quiet outside."

Running upstairs to the kitchen, he barely spared it a glance before he unlocked the kitchen door and stepped outside. A figure swung on him out of the darkness, growling deep in his throat like a dog.

"Dupont," Noir said quietly. "All quiet?"

"Nothing stirring, sir. I'd almost rather a fight."

"Let's hope your wish isn't granted. Keep your ears open." With that, he walked away, beginning a systematic patrol of the inn's environs.

He had good vision at night, and despite the new moon, there was light enough from the sky to make out the path down the cliff to the beach where they had landed. Smugglers had brought them ashore, but they were on their own getting back to the ship. No one lurked below on the beach or on the rocks that he could make out. He just hoped their boat was where they had left it, close into the cliff.

He walked on, hearing and seeing nothing out of the ordinary. If there were soldiers approaching, they were doing so ridiculously quiet. He moved closer to the inn to do another, smaller circle of the building. The light from the coffee room at the front was very faint, showing through a gap in the curtain he hadn't properly closed, or Boucher had made larger by sitting in the window seat. Noir could see his broad back, shifting as it always did when he talked.

Who the devil was he talking to?

*Isabelle de Renarde.* He saw the curve of her arm, even a glimpse of her golden hair, and she leaned forward, listening to Boucher.

What on earth were they talking about?

Ridiculous to be jealous of Boucher. She was an aristocrat, he a child of the revolution. She was the mistress of the unspeakable, undeserving Ashton. A beautiful face and seductive figure were not usually enough to distract him. But she was more. The widow of a traitor, she seemed resigned to the mistrust of her chosen countrymen. And she was deeply unhappy. Grief and loneliness were emotions he could recognize in anyone, for he knew them only too well. But she didn't wear them on her sleeve. He admired her spirit of pride, endurance, and independence. And in earthier matters, he liked the firm, gentle touch of her fingers when she had dressed his wound—which throbbed now that he thought of it.

She smelled divine, too. His arms had ached to close around her fragile, willowy body. He wondered how she would kiss...

*Oh, no, this distraction is becoming too strong. Concentrate on your task, imbecile, and get your men away from here.*

By this time, he had passed the front door and met Dupont going the other way. They nodded to each other, and Noir returned to the kitchen still wondering what on earth Isabelle and Boucher were talking about.

IN FACT, THEY were talking about Noir.

It hadn't started off that way. She'd given him a cup of lukewarm tea, commented on a couple of nasty grazes on his hand, and Boucher had talked about soldiers fighting through injuries, so barely noticing a scratch like his.

"Your captain has a sword wound in his arm from fighting Lieutenant Steele," she observed. "Will that not slow him down if the British soldiers come for you?"

Boucher grinned ferociously. "No. They might get us with sheer numbers, but even then, the captain has a way of getting us out of impossible situations."

"How?" she asked, mostly to keep him talking, to make him comfortable so that he would not notice she was gradually blocking his view of the room. But she was also intrigued and wanted to know.

"Well, there was the time we infiltrated a Spanish-held fort and laid explosives before we were surrounded, and it seemed we had no option but to surrender. But the captain blew it up anyway, with us in it, and in the confusion, every one of us got out and away. Even him. The explosion threw him several yards, but he still flew after us as black as my hat with half his hair singed off."

"But that must have been sheer luck!"

"I thought so, though he claimed he knew from the amount and position of the explosives that our chances were good. Still, that's when they started calling him mad."

"Is he?"

Boucher considered, which was not comforting. "Not mad. Nor even reckless by his own standards. Once, he got us out by letting himself be captured. And then, while the enemy was looking for the rest of us, he overcame his guards and got to us in the nick of time."

"And is that what you do all the time? Crazy raids like this one?"

"Mostly," he admitted. "These days. Would have gone to Russia with the emperor, only Captain le Noir asked for me. He was too injured to go at the time, but they were already planning another incursion into a rebel state in Germany."

"Why do you do it?" she asked curiously. "Why does *he* do it?"

Boucher shrugged. "Orders. I suppose it's more fun than long marches, longer periods sitting on your backside—begging your pardon, madame—and the slog of a pitched battle. What have we got to lose?"

"Forlorn hope," she murmured, remembering to shift her chair just a little closer and hold his gaze.

"Beg your pardon?"

"That's what the British call their volunteers for tasks they're unlikely to survive."

Boucher smiled, just a little fiercely. "There you are then. The captain only leads forlorn hopes."

"Why?"

"He never says. I do know he lost his wife and baby son a couple of years ago. I never knew him before that, so I can't say what he was like then." Boucher's eyes glazed over.

Isabelle sensed movement behind her. More than one person was shifting, quietly, gently. She was sure Boucher would notice, but he was tired and lost in the past, in the comfort of speaking French.

"I saw him once, throw himself over a grenade in a Spanish village. It should have gone off, but it didn't. I don't know why. But just for a moment, I saw his face when he realized it wasn't going to explode. It wasn't relief, or joy, or even astonishment. It was anger."

Isabelle frowned, too startled by this revelation to notice that she'd lost his gaze.

"Here, where are you going?" he demanded, his fingers tightening on the pistol he'd been holding casually across his arm. He leapt to his feet, so Isabelle jumped up, too, bumping into him as the last of the room's occupants bolted into the hall.

He swore at her, shoving her aside as he shot across the room. The shouts of triumph, the draught of icy air, told her the front door was open. Rushing after him, she saw him plough his way through the people at the door.

But that was wrong. They should have been outside by now and running. Someone must have stopped them, another soldier. They'd left one outside, and bad luck had brought him to the wrong place at the wrong time.

And all the soldiers would be running to help their fellows, to restrain their captives once more.

But there was another door.

All they needed was one person free to raise the alarm.

Isabelle turned and ran through the empty kitchen, which was still lit by several lamps. The door to the cellar stairs was wide open as though the men in there had rushed up already to help. And when she lifted the latch of the back door, luck was with her. It opened easily. Someone had forgotten to relock it.

Outside, in the sharp cold of the night, she ran away from the inn, heading for the Finsborough road, where there were cottages just around the next bend.

To her relief, there were no gunshots from the front of the inn. Even the excited shouting had stopped, as though everyone was recaptured with depressing ease. It was little comfort to know that she'd been right, that the Frenchmen were reluctant to shoot. Especially when she became aware it was no longer just her own panting breath, her own pounding footsteps echoing in her ears.

Someone was chasing her and catching up, fast.

She had no time to turn to find out who it was. If she could even see in the dark. In despair, she knew she would never reach the first bend. She tripped over an unseen stone or tree root, but managed to stagger onward with an undignified lurch. Hearing a furious curse behind her, she knew her pursuer had been caught the same way.

Perhaps there was hope after all… Even if she could only scream, it might raise the alarm.

And then something crashed into her back, and she fell forward onto the hard ground.

"Dash it, woman, you run like a hare," Noir panted in her ear.

His full weight was not upon her, but he had both her hands behind her back, and both the intimacy and the indignity outraged her. She did not even have breath to scream.

"Damn you," she gasped as he moved, hauling her to her feet.

"Are you hurt?" he asked curtly.

"No."

"Take a moment to think about it, and then answer. I'm sorry I knocked you down. I thought you were going to scream."

"I was," she said shakily. She took a breath. "For the rest, I expect I am bumped and bruised, but I am not seriously hurt. The others?"

He began to walk, dragging her with him at a fast pace, his hand still gripping both of hers at the base of her spine. "They barely got out the door."

"You will not hurt them, will you?" she said anxiously. "It was my idea."

"I have no time to hurt them," he retorted.

She stared at his profile, which seemed serious, even grim, though that might just have been the darkness. "It will be light soon," she observed. "Why are you still here? You must know the men you seek aren't at the inn."

"I don't know that," he disputed. "In fact, I'm sure they are."

She was silent a moment. "Why did you come in the first place?"

"Why did you?" he countered.

"I don't know now," she said candidly. "A moment of weakness, of longing for something that was never there."

He looked at her then, but it was her turn to look straight ahead. "You will throw him over?"

"I can't throw over what I never had," she snapped. "He is not my lover."

To her surprise, Noir grinned with clear delight.

"It needn't make you so happy," she muttered.

"True," he allowed. "It's none of my business. But I hate to think of you with such a man. What was your husband like?"

She stared at him. "A treacherous bastard. What was your wife like?"

He flinched as though she'd struck him. Yet his grip remained firm on her hands. "So that is what you induced Boucher to talk about. Why?"

"Curiosity. And you haven't answered me."

"She was young and sweet and full of laughter, a perfect antidote for war and cynicism."

"Then perhaps you are the lucky one, and you should stop trying to get yourself killed. Sooner or later, you'll misjudge and your men will die, too."

His gaze remained on her face, though she couldn't make out his expression. They were less than a hundred yards from the inn, and she doubted he would respond. But again, he surprised her. "The aim is never death."

The glow from the building flickered across his lean, unquiet face.

"Then what is?" she asked, almost in despair.

"Distraction," he replied. "I estimate the odds, calculate our ever-changing escape possibilities—in between the action, which is usually more exciting than hunting for elusive, secret rooms."

She blinked. There was no point in asking, *Distraction from what?* "I'm sorry we couldn't provide more entertainment."

"Don't be. You are, you must know, the biggest distraction of all."

She eyed him warily. "Is that a compliment?"

"Not when you also distract Boucher, a far more deliberate dis-tract—" Abruptly, he broke off, staring at her, though she doubted he was seeing her. "The taproom," he said inexplicably.

He released one of her hands, dragging her forward by the other as he all but ran into the inn, slamming and locking the door behind him. "Boucher!" he yelled. "Lefevre! The taproom! Bring the innkeeper!"

"What in the world…" she began, both baffled and amused. Nei-ther were emotions she had imagined would come with her recapture.

"And the axe!" Noir yelled, more worryingly.

Since no one told her not to, she followed Noir into the taproom. He walked around it, stamping on various areas of floor. It was almost funny, except for the serious, focused look on his face.

Caron entered the room, saying, "We've got everyone back and the extra keys."

Noir barely acknowledged it. "How carefully did you search in here?"

"Not very, I suppose. We dug up a couple of floorboards," he added as one snapped up under Noir's stamping foot. "There was nothing. Checked the cupboards."

By then, Boucher had appeared with a large axe in one hand, Mr. Villin in the other. The innkeeper looked bemused.

"Sit here, Mr. Villin," Noir said, almost jovially, placing a wooden chair for him in the middle of the room.

Villin sat without fuss, blinking up at his captor. The other captives began to squeeze in behind Boucher, Lefevre and his pistol behind them. Noir was not so focused that he didn't cast them more than a quick glance, counting them, Isabelle was sure.

"Mr. Villin," Noir said, taking the axe from Boucher, "I know your secret room is accessed from here."

"I don't see how you can know anything so nonsensical," Villin replied with dignity.

"If there's no access from the main cellar, it makes sense for it to be close to where you serve the illicit brandy. And then, you were quite eager to keep fetching people brandy. I think your secret room is also a way out, and you planned to use it to escape and raise the alarm."

Villin scratched his head. "I wish I'd thought of it. I'd have built one special."

"Oh, I think you did. You or your predecessors." He began to walk, bumping the axe head on the floor as he went. "And you're going to tell me where it is. Am I close yet?" He hit the axe handle against the front wall, under the window.

Villin watched him with the same wide-eyed astonishment as he walked around the room, occasionally crossing the floor toward him. All the time, Noir watched Villin's face rather than where he was going or what he was doing. More than once, someone had to get out of his way, and twice he walked into a table, but nothing deflected him, even when he went behind the counter and tapped the inner wall with his axe a couple of times. Moving back, he bumped into the counter and paused.

"Now, I'm close," he said softly.

"Close to the brandy," Villin agreed.

For some reason, although this whole pantomime seemed an exercise in futility, Isabelle found she was holding her breath.

Noir walked back the way he had come, still watching Villin's face. At the end of the counter, he turned and walked the entire length of it, almost rhythmically tapping the axe against the internal wall as he went.

"No," he murmured. "Not quite." Coming around the counter, he walked in front of Villin, tapping his axe on the floor. Just past him, he halted and lifted the axe. Instead of dropping it on the floor, he swung it casually sideways so it bumped against the counter, as if by accident. "Here."

With that, he turned, swung the axe in earnest, and hacked into the counter. And a door in it swung open. Gasping, Isabelle hurried forward to see…more wood.

"I blocked it up," Villin said. "Too many ruffians knew where it was. Wasn't safe for my family to have it there anymore. Nor for my guests. Can't be used at all now."

"Maybe," Noir said, dropping to a crouch. Laying down the axe, he felt around the wood and heaved. It came away easily in his hand in one, large plank. In fact, it looked as if it had once been a taproom table. "Light," he commanded.

Hastily, Caron jumped up and brought the lamp. And by its glow, Isabelle saw a small chamber some three feet below the level of the floor. In it, sat four men, bound and gagged, eyes blinking madly in the sudden light.

# CHAPTER SIX

"**W**ELL, I'LL BE damned," Sir Maurice murmured, clearly amused.

"My God," Caron said in an awed voice, "he was right. I should have known he was right."

The men, meanwhile, ungagged and unbound, were heaved into the body of the taproom and helped to the bench under the window.

Noir glared at Villin, who was pouring out mugs of small beer for them. "Is that any way to treat human beings?"

Villin glared back. "I could have let them out long before this if you hadn't turned up!"

"Bah," Noir uttered, turning to the French prisoners. "Drink up, my friends. We have a boat to catch. Caron, fetch Dupont, we're leaving."

However, before he'd finished speaking, the fourth man came running into the taproom, skidding to a halt before his captain. "Soldiers on the way!"

"Damnation, could they could not have held off for five minutes? How far and how many?"

"Can't see them yet, just hear them, but I'd say about ten on horseback on the road from Finsborough. Five minutes?"

"Then let's go."

"You'll walk straight into them," Sir Maurice said with some satisfaction.

"Nah," Villin contradicted. "They're on the road. The captain here will leave by boat, if I'm not much mistaken."

"They'll shoot you out of the water," said Lieutenant Steele.

"Only by luck, and that commodity appears to be with us." He swung on the still dazed prisoners. "Come, time to go."

One instinctively tried to obey and fell back into his seat. His legs didn't appear to work.

"They're in no state to go anywhere yet," Isabelle said. "You must go without them."

"I won't," Noir said flatly.

"Then stay and be captured with them."

He stared at her, then at the escaped prisoners, and dragged his hand through his hair. "Come on, my friends, wiggle those arms and legs. Let's practice walking. Two more minutes and then we leave."

But it seemed Dupont has misjudged, for Isabelle could already hear the clattering of approaching hooves.

Noir swore under his breath. "Make sure the doors are locked. Dupont, you and Caron make sure they don't surround us. Lefevre, watch the prisoners."

*Dear God, are they going to fight here?* Isabelle sank down on a bench and discovered Sir Maurice beside her. He patted her hand in what he clearly imagined was a comforting manner. Isabelle found it excessively annoying and jumped up again, following Noir to the window. "Captain! You cannot mean to let the inn be besieged? Assaulted? It will be a terrible waste of life! Think of the fam—"

"You are, of course, quite right," Noir agreed. He was peering out of the window, where the darkness was breaking up with lantern light. Rummaging in his pocket, he came up with a large handkerchief.

"Then what do you mean to do?" she demanded.

"Create a way out," he replied. "Please, sit here."

Frowning, she sat, watching him tie the handkerchief around the head of the axe. Then, he reached up to the window latch, unlocking it. He paused and glanced down at her. "Actually, you might want to stand behind me, or sit on the floor until I establish if they will talk."

"I shall stay where I am," she said instinctively. Partly, it was pride, but somewhere, it crossed her mind that the English soldiers were unlikely to shoot him if a lady was visible beside him.

A frown flickered on his brow. But in the end, he turned away, opened the window a crack, and edged out his handkerchief on the end of the axe.

"Sir!" someone called outside in an excited voice.

"Don't shoot it, fool," came the irritated response. A horse clopped nearer until a soldier came into view, a middle-aged officer. Behind him and to either side, were three subordinate soldiers, rifles aimed at the window. "Do I take it this is your sign of surrender?"

"Truce," Noir corrected and opened the window further. "While you and I talk, my men will not shoot yours, if none of you shoot at us."

"And whom am I addressing, sir?"

"Captain le Noir. Apparently, I am a *forlorn hope*, along with my men. But I do not believe the hope is so forlorn that we cannot discuss matters as officers of honor."

"I am Captain Brandon. What do you wish to discuss?"

"Safe passage away from here."

"You must see that I am unlikely to grant such a request. You are an enemy soldier in my country. And I believe you have with you some escaped prisoners-of-war."

Noir spared a moment to scowl at Villin. *"Now, I do."*

The English officer paused, peering beyond Noir for the first time. "You have people, civilians in there. Is anyone hurt? Dead?"

"I regret the injury of one Lieutenant Steele of the Royal Navy who bravely drew his sword on me. He should live, although I would advise he see a surgeon. Also present are several civilians, including a young family, the innkeeper and his family, a gentleman who claims acquaintance with your Prince Regent, and this lady at my side. I beg you will consider them when deciding whether to grant my request."

Even over this distance, Captain Brandon's scowl was dire. "Are you telling me you will use these people as hostages?"

"No," Noir said in apparent surprise. "I am telling you they are here, and that if you shoot at us, you will put them in danger, too. I will also say, I have no desire to shoot at you."

"Then throw down your weapons and come out. You will be treated with honor."

Noir sighed. "That is my problem. I do not think I can walk willingly into a prison. Here is my proposal, sir. My men and I will come out with Lieutenant Steele and all the civilians." He gestured above him. "Except for the family in their chamber. You will see they are safe and look after them. Then, my men, your one-time prisoners, and I, shall leave your shores and—er—never trouble you again."

Captain Brandon was silent, perhaps flabbergasted by the effrontery. At last he said, "You must know I could never agree to that."

"But consider the alternative, my friend. We fight. Some of us die or are injured, the inn is destroyed…and some of the casualties will inevitably be civilians. You do remember the lady and the friend of the Prince Regent?"

"Only too well!" the officer snapped. "I will promise to treat you and your men with all honor, but beyond that, I cannot go."

Noir smiled. "Then find me someone who can. For I have grown fond of my prisoners here and have no wish to see them die. Shall we make a truce of one hour while you decide?"

Captain Brandon stared at him a little wildly, as though wondering how they had got to this point. "One hour," he said at last. "Or less, after further discussion."

"Agreed," Noir said cheerfully and closed the window.

"You are utterly without conscience!" Isabelle burst out.

Noir sighed. "Perhaps. But I am trying to keep us all alive. You don't imagine they will really let us live, do you? Soldiers with no uniform on enemy soil?"

Isabelle closed her mouth. It was something that had never occurred to her. Even if the officer outside meant what he said, the matter would soon be out of his hands.

Steele, who had limped through with Lily, exclaimed, "You know full well they can never agree to your terms!"

Noir shrugged. "I know they won't want to. But what is the alternative? To storm the inn? If that happens, I can make you as secure as possible in the cellar, or in Mr. Villin's secret room under the counter. But that will not necessarily save you all. People will die."

"You could give yourself up," Ashton drawled. "And save all our lives."

"I need to get my men home. And the prisoners."

"Offer yourself, for God's sake! They might let your minions survive."

"They might," Noir said dubiously. "But no, while I shall bear your plan in mind, I prefer mine."

"It won't work," Steele said flatly.

"We shall see. We have an hour to prepare. Mr. Villin, I regret we have to further disturb your inn for our defenses. Stout tables across the windows and doors and so on. You know your inn best. If they fire it, where is safest for you and these people?"

Villin, clearly dismayed, did not look at him but at his wife and daughter. In silence, Lily dragged her gaze free and glanced around at everyone, lingering on Isabelle and then Noir, who was already upending a table and clearly considering whether or not to chop off its legs with the axe.

"Dad," she said. "They aren't bad men. In France, somewhere, we probably have people doing much the same thing."

Villin scowled. "But then what did I keep the damned prisoners for? We'll be accused of abetting the enemy—and we'll be guilty!"

Noir lowered his axe, frowning at the innkeeper. "If you have an alternative solution, my friend, please tell, because I won't deny I don't care for my own plan above half."

Villin considered, glancing at his own regulars, Sir Maurice, Isabelle, and Lieutenant Steele, and fixed his gaze once more on his wife and daughter. He sighed and met Noir's gaze. "The secret room is...well, it's more than that."

"Is it, by God?" Noir dropped his axe and walked toward the innkeeper. "How much more?"

"A lot. It's a secret passage that leads down inside the cliff to the beach."

One of the French prisoners swore. The others exchanged glances of frustration and fury. They had been within easy distance of escape and had never known it.

Noir grinned. "Monsieur, I could kiss you."

"I beg you won't!" Villin growled, but Noir was already scowling again.

"I see your problem," he murmured. "You will be in trouble for helping us escape. Since obviously I did not know this route when I confronted the officer outside. Either way, I am responsible."

Isabelle drew in a breath. "What if we keep the prisoners you came for? You take your men home. We keep them."

"No," Noir said flatly.

"Unacceptable!" Steele snapped.

"Compromise," Isabelle retorted, swinging to face him. "Villin and his family are the heroes who risked themselves to recapture dangerous French prisoners, and if their rescue party got away, well that is unfortunate. We cannot be expected to fight both with no weapons. If the prisoners are still here, there can be no possibility of collusion between us and Captain le Noir. And the captain and his men live to fight another day."

"It strikes me," Steele said bitterly, "that our country would benefit more from clapping up Noir and his cohorts and letting the prisoners go free!"

To her surprise, Noir seemed to consider that, too. Then he strode over to the bewildered prisoners. A low, rapid discussion followed. It was too quiet for Isabelle to make out the words over the loud arguments of everyone else.

Then Noir yelled, "Quiet!" And as the noise cut off like a slamming door, he said fiercely, "It is decided." His eyes were as furious as his voice. Clearly, he was not happy with the decision. "The prisoners stay—for now. We go by the secret passage, and we take hostages, Mr. Villin to open his blocked passage, and Madame de Renarde in case we are followed or meet resistance at the other end of the passage. The Prince Regent's friend, here, will stay as protection to everyone else. Lieutenant Steele, I need your word of agreement."

"Mine?" Steele exclaimed. "Why?"

"Because someone will need to make sure no one else gives the game away to the soldiers outside. And to ensure everyone lives."

"Sir, you put me in an impossible position," Steele objected. "I don't want you to escape! And besides, I am injured."

A smile flickered in Noir's angry eyes. "Excuse," he retorted. "You are more than capable. And you do know this is the only way to be sure no one dies."

"How can we be sure?" Sir Maurice demanded. "You're taking Madame de Renarde and Villin away from us. You could slit their throats, drown them—"

"Don't be an idiot, sir," Isabelle snapped. "Why would he be taking such care of our lives only to slit our throats?"

There was no reasonable answer to that. It was probably a better question to ask why he was taking such care in the first place. This reckless soldier, so careless of his own life...

"Go," Steele said angrily.

Noir drew the naked sword from his belt—Steele's sword—and

presented it to him hilt first. "It has been an honor, Lieutenant."

Steele blinked. A reluctant smile began to dawn. "You'll forgive me if I say I hope we never meet again."

Noir's lips twisted. He bowed and turned away, exchanging a long look with the resigned prisoners. He sighed. "Forgive me. I regret this more than I can say." He drew his own sword and seized Isabelle by the arm. "Behold, I drive the innkeeper and Madame Renarde before me at sword-point. Remember. Villin, lead the way."

# CHAPTER SEVEN

IMPATIENTLY, NOIR REACHED up from the secret room floor, seized her by the waist, and swung her down. He barely looked at her as he urged her after Villin through another hidden door, which the innkeeper had just unblocked, and which revealed a passage.

By the poor light of the bobbing lanterns, Isabelle could make out Noir's permanent scowl, but more than that, his very tension told her how much he hated this failure to bring the prisoners home. There was nothing she could say to make him feel better about that. In time, surely, he would appreciate more that he was saving the freedom, and even the lives of his men and preventing inevitable casualties among the civilians.

"Thank you," she blurted, when she could stay silent no longer. The close, dank passage downward had turned into rough-hewn steps, and he turned, seizing her hand once more to prevent her tumbling down.

"For what?" he demanded bitterly. "Holding you at gunpoint for several hours and using you as a shield against my enemies?"

"For accepting a solution that goes against your...code."

He made a sound very like a snort. But he still held her hand. His was rough in texture, its grip firm but not hard, certainly not violent.

"Will your superiors be angry with you?"

He shrugged. "Everyone fails sometimes. There is always more to do. What of you? What of your life?"

"I think I shall become a governess. I was a kind of unofficial one before to a family member. I rather enjoyed it, although admittedly, I was a somewhat privileged governess."

"Can't you be so again to the same child?"

"Alas, no. She no longer lives with my cousins. And besides, the cousins no longer speak to me."

"Why not?"

"Because my husband was betraying their country."

He said nothing for a moment. Then he said intensely, "Life is unbearable for you here."

"Life can be unpleasant. But we both know very little is actually unbearable."

He stopped, holding up Caron who was behind them. The rest of his men were ahead with Villin and seemed to have reached the end of the passage, for the sound of stone being pounded drifted up to her, along with a fine, unpleasant dust. Villin's final blockage was being undone. She just hoped there were no soldiers waiting on the beach to seize them as they emerged.

She doubted Noir or his men would go with them quietly.

"Go on," he said impatiently to Caron, and as the soldier squeezed past and vanished with his light, he added abruptly, "Life should not be like that. Simply *borne*. Endured."

And suddenly, for no reason, there were tears in her throat. She couldn't remember the last time she had wept. "Isn't that what you do, too?" she fought back. "We just have different methods. What else are your *distractions*?"

He stared up at her from the step below. By the pale light that penetrated around the bend in the passage, she couldn't make out his expression, just a faint glittering of the eyes. He moved up to her step, too close, too intimate.

"It shouldn't be like that," he whispered. "Not for either of us. With you…" He broke off and a breath of laughter brushed her cheek.

"How maddening to meet you here, like this... You give me hope, Isabelle de Renarde."

The emotion crowding in her throat broke free. She didn't want to leave him with nothing, and yet even as the words came to her with wonder, she recognized they were truth. "As you give to me," she gasped.

His head dipped, touching his warm forehead to hers. His free hand cupped her face, and she squeezed her eyes shut with shame because he'd found the dampness of her tears.

"Come with me, Isabelle," he said urgently. "Come home."

Her eyes snapped open, and she drew her head back against the wall, staring at him. "What?" she whispered.

His mouth came down on hers, sudden, tender, and so sweet, she didn't even try to avoid it. Dormant desire surged within her, crashing into her helpless tangle of emotion, melting into it for one long, beautiful moment.

*Come home.* "I can't." she whispered against his lips. "You know I can't."

"Renarde did not betray *my* country. You would be a heroine there."

Laughter caught in her throat. "No, I wouldn't. This is the only country I've ever known." It wasn't quite true, but it was close enough. "Go, you madman. You will be grateful to me one day."

"I'm grateful to you now."

From below came the urgent call of one of his men. "Captain! We're through."

"I'm coming," he said impatiently. "Check for any welcome party." Even then, he released her very slowly.

"Take care of your life," she said unsteadily.

A smile flickered across his lips. "Take care of your happiness." And with that, he leapt down the rest of the steps, and she could hear his voice, speaking to his men.

Isabelle followed more slowly. She stood amongst the rubble in the cave, beside Villin, watching as the Frenchmen pulled a boat from the shadows and dragged it down the beach to the water. They clambered in without so much as a backward glance.

Well, they would hardly wave as if this was parting of good friends. It would ruin the hostage tale. Still, she would have liked him to look back at her, just once.

She shivered, touching her lips, remembering his kiss, the temptation. *Come home.*

"It will be light in half an hour," Villin observed as they rowed into the gloom. "They'll be sitting ducks."

"I wonder where their ship is? They can't row all the way to France."

"I don't suppose we'll ever know." He sighed. "Well, I kept my prisoners and saved my inn—most of my inn. I suppose I can go back and face the music. Before I block up this damned passage again."

She turned, picked up one of the lanterns, and preceded him through the cave.

BREAKFAST AT THE Hart was not something Isabelle had even considered. Climbing wearily back through the secret passage, she had been conscious, mainly, of a desire to sleep, but at the first wafting smells of frying bacon as she entered the house, she realized she was starving.

By then, of course, the inn was overrun with soldiers. Lieutenant Steele had summoned them as soon as Isabelle and Villin had returned but, removing any need for Steele to lie by more than omission, it was she who had told the harrowing tale of being forced through the horrid, steep, winding passage to be used, if necessary, as human shields.

Captain Brandon had immediately sent half his men through the passage and raced over ground to the beach with the other half. But neither party had seen any sign of the French raiders. From the inn window as day began to break, Isabelle had glimpsed a few distant vessels at sea, a couple of smaller dots closer to shore. Impossible to know if Noir and his men were in one of those dots or heading for any of the visible ships.

By the time Brandon returned, fuming, the dots seemed to have vanished. Any suspicions which the British officer might have harbored were clearly shoved aside as he and his men—along with the French prisoners—tucked into bacon, eggs, and sausages, with thick slices of newly baked bread and butter. They were served in the coffee room, while Isabelle, along with Sir Maurice, Lieutenant Steele, and the Ferris family, ate in the private parlor.

At first, Sir Maurice had bridled at being asked to share the parlor he had hired with anyone except Isabelle, until she had pointed out, in Lily's hearing, that it would be most improper for her to breakfast alone with him. And that the alternative was for her to join Captain Brandon and the soldiers.

"How are the prisoners?" she asked Lily as the girl poured coffee for them all.

Lily shrugged a little sadly. "They seem quite resigned with my mother's breakfast inside them. I think the adventure of escape quickly palled, even before my father rumbled them and got his friends to bundle them into…the place they were. Are you sure you want coffee, madame? Wouldn't you like to sleep? The chamber is yours until tomorrow with no extra charge, and we've already set it back in order."

"No, the notion to sleep has quite left me," Isabelle replied. She felt Ashton's gaze on her face but refused to look at him. Now that the excitement was over, she felt hunted. And not in a pleasant way. Ashton didn't admire her. He wanted admiration for possessing her. Whether he was like that with all women, or just with her, the contemptible wife of the traitor, she did not know.

She did know she couldn't tolerate it. Last night, meeting the reckless, perceptive, compassionate Noir had cleared her mind and returned her to some level of self-respect. She would not compound her mistakes with Pierre and Verne with any worse ones.

"Lady Overton's ball is on Friday," Sir Maurice pointed out. He smiled at his own cleverness. "I assumed that was why you had come down to Sussex."

"On the contrary, I have not been invited to Lady Overton's. I had hoped to see my family, but the time isn't convenient. I shall return to London."

"You must allow me to escort you."

"Thank you, that won't be necessary. I intend to call on friends first, and I would not keep you from the Overtons' ball." She said it as an excuse to avoid him, but as the words spilled out, she realized that it was what she wanted to do. Verne *was* her friend, whatever he had been in the past. And his wife could be. Besides, Jane was with them now, and it was the child, not her Longstone grandparents, that Isabelle was eager to see again.

AN HOUR LATER, refreshed and dressed in a cleaner if older gown, pelisse and bonnet, she opened her bedchamber door for Jem, the stable hand, to carry it down to her waiting carriage. Then, dragging her gaze away from the expanse of sea in her window, she picked up her reticule and her traveling cloak.

"Isabelle."

She turned to see Sir Maurice in the doorway. "Goodbye, sir. I'm sure we'll meet again in London."

He took a step into the room. "Again? Isabelle, we didn't exactly *meet* here."

So, it was not to be a matter of discreet and subtle hints. She met his gaze. "Sir Maurice, my coming here was the most foolish thing I have ever done, whatever my reputation may say to the contrary. I find I am grateful to our late captors for preventing any passage between us, and more than anything else that tells me any sort of liaison between us would be wrong. I am sorry to have misled you."

He frowned. The corner of his eye twitched. "Misled me? My dear lady, this was your idea. You owe me."

She stared at him. "The Hart was my idea. The invitation, if you recall, was yours. But you are right. I do owe you. For indiscretion, rudeness, and a quite ungentlemanly lack of respect. Be grateful I have not paid this debt. And pray I never do."

His mouth was an ugly sneer. With his heel, he kicked the bed-chamber door shut and took a step toward her.

But the door did not close. It bounced off someone's hand—Jem. "This all your luggage, ma'am?" he said cheerfully.

"Yes, thank you, Jem," she replied and sailed out before either of them.

Discretion was indeed the better part of valor. But part of her longed still to plant her knee hard where he would least appreciate it. She was not as helpless as he imagined.

SHE DIRECTED THE hired coachman to Finmarsh House. It was not a long journey, but long enough for her newfound confidence to plummet. She had no real reason to believe that the Vernes would receive her when her own cousins did not. She almost stopped the carriage twice to instruct the driver to turn onto the main London road. After all, the sooner she returned to London, the sooner she could begin her search for a governess position.

But she sat on her hands to prevent her rapping on the ceiling. She had come this far. She might as well find out once and for all.

She stepped down from the coach with as much leisurely regality as she could muster and sailed up the steps to the front door. At least the footman who opened it hadn't been instructed to refuse her entry. He showed her to the reception room and carried her card on a silver tray across the hall in the direction of what had once been Verne's library.

Isabelle sat on the edge of the uncomfortable chair, preparing not to care if she were denied. In the end, she did not have much time, for the footman returned almost immediately, not to dismiss her but to ask her to please follow him. She was led through the library—which looked somehow brighter and airier than it used to—and into the room beyond.

Her feet almost faltered as she followed the footman, for this, as she well knew, used to be Verne's bedchamber.

It wasn't anymore. It was a bright, warm sitting room with several comfortable chairs and sofas and a writing desk at the window from which the elegant figure of Lady Cecily rose to greet her.

"Isabelle," she said, smiling and holding out her hand in welcome. "What a pleasant surprise. I did not know you were in Sussex."

Isabelle took her hand, hiding her relief. "It was an impulsive decision. I hope I haven't interrupted you. I just called to inquire after you both. And Jane."

"How kind of you! Please, sit and I shall ring for…what would you like? Tea? Sherry? You will stay for luncheon, I hope? Patrick and Jane are out on the estate, but they shouldn't be long."

Lady Cecily had always possessed natural manners that endeared her to all but the highest sticklers. And since she was the daughter of a duke, she did not need care much for such trivial disapproval.

Isabelle chose a chair on one side of the fireplace. "I would love to stay and see them, but you should know, I have eaten the most enormous breakfast at the Hart and will be able to live off it comfortably for several more days."

Cecily laughed and broke off to order tea. "We'll have the wine when Verne gets back, then. But did you say you were at the Hart? What on earth was going on there this morning?"

"You heard?" Isabelle exclaimed. "Already?"

"One of the maids had it from the stable lad that some escaped French prisoners were recaptured there. But the dairy maid said it was smugglers they caught and that Villin's been clapped up in Finsborough jail, which I sincerely hope is not true."

"So do I! But he was hale and hearty and ordering his taproom when I saw him last."

"Then it is all a hum?" Cecily asked.

"Not *all*. The soldiers did arrive at an ungodly hour of the morning to recapture the escaped prisoners—who were being hidden by the Villins from a French raiding party who had come ashore to collect them!"

Cecily's mouth fell open. "And you were in the middle of all this? I don't know whether that is wildly exciting or simply terrifying!"

"Neither do I," Isabelle admitted.

"You must be wishing you had not stopped there but gone on to the Longstones."

Isabelle hesitated. Fortunately, the tea arrived, and she did not need to say anything until the servants had departed.

"I thought I would speak to Jane—and to you—before I called there. To be frank, Elvira made it plain that I was not welcome in their home after Pierre...well, you know."

"Only too well, but Pierre's sins are hardly to be laid at your door."

"She may have changed her mind," Isabelle said with forced lightness. "But you will know better than I. Please don't spare my feelings. I am quite inured."

A rueful smile flickered over Cecily's face. "Actually, we are not on visiting terms with the Longstones. Miss Arbor takes Jane to see her grandmother for tea every second Sunday, but that is the only contact."

"I see." Isabelle searched her face. "Do you regret it?" she asked carefully.

"Not in the slightest. It was my decision."

"Good for you. They were vile to Patrick."

"Viler than you know," Cecily said grimly. "But it is too pleasant a day to dwell on the past."

As Isabelle agreed, she became aware of a slamming door some-where in the house and voices approaching—a deep, unmistakable voice belonging to Patrick Verne and another higher and more childish one that made Isabelle smile with pleasure. Their laughter grew nearer along with pounding feet, and they launched themselves into the room almost together.

"I won, Cecily, I won!" Jane claimed. Then as her gleeful eyes fell on Isabelle, they widened. "Cousin Izzy!" she cried and flew to her with a hug guaranteed to melt the hardest of hearts. For the second time that day, Isabelle wanted to weep.

Lord Verne's laughing welcome was more restrained but equally natural. It wasn't that either he—or his wife—had forgotten the liaison. Merely, it was not important to them as they were now. Cecily was secure enough to lose her jealousy. And Patrick happy enough that he looked at no other woman as he did his wife. Isabelle, once unsure how she would feel about that, found herself relaxing into their company. By the time luncheon was served, she was genuinely glad for their happiness, and her ache of loss so faint as to be an echo. Everyone had moved on; everything had changed.

Of course, she had to tell the story of the raiders and the soldiers again. And if Patrick and Cecily guessed she was not telling everything, they did not press her.

It was Jane who changed the subject by informing her with great eagerness that on Friday, she was going to stay the night with Eliza

Maybury.

"I'm very glad to hear it," Isabelle said, genuinely delighted that Jane had developed such a friendship.

"Because of the ball," Cecily explained. "We'll come home, of course, but rather than wake Jane at three o'clock in the morning, we'll leave her there. It will be nice for Eliza to have company, too, when the rest of the family is occupied. Are you staying with the Overtons?"

"Oh, no, I shall be back in London," Isabelle replied. "I have quite decided to be a governess."

While the Vernes digested this, Jane eyed her dubiously. "Will you teach them watercolor painting and etiquette?"

"Whatever I am required to."

"Uncle Patrick thought you had forgotten history and Latin and—"

"Did he?" Isabelle interrupted. "Or did he think I didn't know them in the first place?"

Patrick only grinned at her. "I didn't work out until later that you were teaching only what Elvira wanted Jane to know. But you slipped in the odd nugget of knowledge, I've since discovered."

"I'm overwhelmed by your notice," Isabelle said wryly.

After lunch, they walked in the garden that had once been beautifully formal under the ownership of Patrick's late sister-in-law, and then wild and neglected under his. Now, with Cecily in charge, it seemed natural and pleasant without being overgrown.

"Before you take up drudgery," Cecily said lightly, "why do you not stay with us for a few days? In fact, come to the ball with us."

Touched in spite of herself, Isabelle said with difficulty, "I have not been invited by Lady Overton." She smiled, as though it were funny. "And to be frank, if I have to hire the carriage for any longer, I won't be able to eat once I return to London."

"Well, that would hardly be fair. Patrick will pay him off and you can go back in our carriage."

Isabelle searched her face and opted for honesty. "I will happily spend a couple of days with you if you truly wish it. But I have some pride, and I will not inflict myself on Lady Overton who is too good natured to ask me to leave."

"Oh, they have servants well-trained to deal with that kind of thing," Patrick said, overhearing. "If she didn't want you there, then you wouldn't get near her or her guests."

"Exactly. So tomorrow or Friday would be a good day for me to return to London."

"Let me speak to her," Cecily advised. "I am sure lack of invitation was a mere oversight. In fact, you are probably included on the Longstones' card."

"Cecily, you are sweet," Isabelle said helplessly. "But I do not *wish* to be invited, particularly not as a favor to someone else."

"It wouldn't be," Patrick said. "You're being too proud."

"Pride is all I have," she said lightly.

"Then don't misuse it," he retorted. "Isabelle, you are young and beautiful and charming, and the Overtons don't believe for a minute that you were involved in Pierre's treachery."

"I think this is just what you need to get back out into society," Cecily agreed.

Isabelle looked from one to the other. "Why should I want to do that? To be a more discontented governess than otherwise? Or to meet likely employers?"

Cecily shrugged. "Or to forego the need of employment at all. Who knows? You might encounter the love of your life there."

Isabelle laughed. "Are you matchmaking already, Cecily? Even were I not so recently widowed, I am now entirely unmarriageable. Poor, foreign, and the widow of a traitor. Write to me and tell me all about the ball."

# CHAPTER EIGHT

ARMAND LE NOIR woke quite suddenly from his deep if troubled sleep. It was still light beyond the porthole on the smuggler's ship, so he couldn't have slept very long. But he knew he'd wakened for a reason. A reason more than the contented snoring of his men on the cabin floor.

He sat up, rubbing his face to bring back life and thought.

*Isabelle.* He had kissed Isabelle, and against all odds, she had kissed him back.

She hadn't gone with him, though. If she had, he wouldn't have had this crazy idea. He would have taken her to safety. Frowning with the effort of remembrance, he went to speak to the crew, who were a mixture of nationalities.

It was the English first mate he wanted. "Higgins," he greeted him, sitting him bodily down on the bench on deck. "What did you tell me last night? About where they'd taken the French prisoners?"

"Finsborough jail. A few miles inland. They've to wait there until they're picked up by the prison guards—their punishment for losing them in the first place, I suppose."

"It took our boys three days to get down to Finsborough on foot," Noir mused. "How long would it take soldiers?"

"Riding? Half that. Although of course, word has to get back to the prison for them to come. So, I suppose that makes it about three days at least. Why? What difference does it make?"

Noir's breath caught. "Every difference in the world. Five men can't rescue four prisoners from a guarded fort. But they can probably break them out of a country jail. Turn the ship back to England."

Higgins laughed at him.

So did the captain, until Noir pulled out his pistol and held it to his head.

"You're insane!" Higgins yelled.

"Want to test that?" Noir inquired.

"No," the captain growled. "Do as he damn well says!"

Boucher, emerging onto the deck yawning and scratching, stopped dead at the sight of his captain holding his pistol to the head of the smuggler chief while the rest of the crew seemed to be running around, changing sails and shouting.

Boucher groaned. "We're going back, aren't we? And these cut-throats won't wait for us again now that you've provoked them! To call it no worse."

"Nonsense. We just have to pay them enough."

"And how in hell do we do that?" Boucher demanded.

"Oh, we'll think of something," Noir said happily. "Highway robbery, perhaps!"

Uneasily, Boucher believed him.

ISABELLE DID NOT have to wait long to discover who Cecily had picked out as a possible husband.

Lord Torbridge, once the chief suitor of Lady Cecily herself, arrived during the afternoon to stay until after the ball.

On the face of it, he was a strange, even bizarre match to even consider. For one thing, although good natured and pleasingly humorous, he was a high stickler for propriety and even before Pierre's treachery was discovered, Isabelle had been considered somewhat fast. And then, there was the small point that he was one of the two people who had shot Pierre and killed him. Not that Isabelle objected to that, and it was certainly not common knowledge, but she couldn't help wondering how Torbridge would be able to reconcile the killing with marrying the widow.

The puzzle was merely academic, of course, since neither she nor Torbridge, she was sure, were considering marriage. But somehow, during that evening, it seemed to become accepted that she would go to the Overtons' ball.

In fact, after dinner as they left the gentlemen to their wine and repaired to the drawing room, a footman brought Cecily a letter, which she opened at once. Another note fell from inside, and when Isabelle picked it up, she saw this one was addressed to her.

Cecily cast her a flickering smile and sat down. "From Lady Overton," she said. "I wrote to her in the afternoon. She would be delighted to receive you tomorrow evening and only apologizes for the oversight. I imagine your letter says the same thing."

It did. And Isabelle, already beguiled by her pleasant day in the company of people who were, against the odds, her friends, gave in to the inevitable and resolved to write her acceptance in the morning.

Jane, who had come to the drawing room for an hour before bed, clapped her hands with glee. "Then I can help you dress, too!"

"I did not bring a ball gown," Isabelle said. "So, you must help me dress up something else so that no one will notice."

Jane retired to bed, full of impossibly splendid plans.

"She is thriving under your care," Isabelle observed. "I'm glad. She was too…isolated with my cousin."

"Well, you must know I bestow respectability on Verne," Cecily said wryly, "so she is certainly less isolated than she would have been."

Something about her voice or her eyes made Isabelle say, "And you, Cecily? Will there be a child of your own?"

Cecily's face broke into smiles. Her arm moved instinctively across her abdomen. "How did you guess?"

"It isn't difficult, and I am thrilled for you both." Oddly, it was the truth. "When do you expect this interesting event?"

"Early spring, we think."

"An excellent time to bring new life into the world. But Cecily," she added, hearing the door open in the dining room and Verne's voice raised in laughing dispute. "You are barking up the wrong tree with Torbridge."

"Oh, I don't know. I always felt there was more to him than met the eye. Like with you." She sighed. "You sound very certain."

"I am."

"I suppose it has only been a few months since—"

"To be frank, I have felt like a widow for years," Isabelle interrupted. "I do not miss Pierre. I do not even mourn Pierre, for I did that years ago, too. And there's no need to look at me like that either, for my reluctance has nothing to do with Verne."

Cecily blinked and then laughed. "I always liked you for your directness," she observed. "So, who does it have to do with?"

Isabelle opened her mouth to deride the idea that it was to do with anyone but her. Only the dark, intense face of Armand le Noir swam behind her eyes, and her heart seemed to melt into her stomach when she remembered his kiss.

This was silly. Schoolroom girl silly.

Cecily had begun to look intrigued, but fortunately Verne and Torbridge strolled into the drawing room and distracted her.

Cecily was right, of course. There was more to Torbridge than met the eye. A lot more. He hadn't just happened to be in the right place to prevent Pierre killing Verne earlier in the year. And Isabelle was reminded of this as the evening progressed and he casually worked the conversation around to last night's troubles at the inn. And he was clearly aware that Villin had captured and hidden the French prisoners.

"Now that I think about it," she said with a frown, "that was really odd of him. Why hide them like that?"

"Because I asked him to," Torbridge replied unexpectedly. He smiled faintly. "We intercepted some communication between particular prisoners and…let us say channels that lead to France. So, we let these men escape in the hope of intercepting those who came to meet them."

"To learn more about these channels?" Isabelle hazarded.

"Yes. And also, perhaps, to infiltrate this channel, to have our own man there. It is an important time for us. Bonaparte's Russian adventure leaves France vulnerable as it has never been since he came to power. We must utilize every possibility. Unfortunately, everything moved faster than we expected. I had thought it more likely the prisoners would be met on the Cornish coast, and by the time Villin's message reached me, it was just too late to catch everyone together. To be fair, Villin didn't know that I was more interested in the rescuers than the escapees."

His gaze developed that unexpected sharpness she had seen before, even while his lips smiled with perfect amiability. "What did you think of Captain le Noir? Is he a man appreciative of the finer things of life?"

Isabelle blinked. "If you mean can he be bribed into betrayal, I would very much doubt it!"

Torbridge merely shrugged and changed the subject, and yet several times he came back to it, as though trying to piece together the puzzle that was Captain le Noir. Isabelle knew how he felt.

"Damn, it's the mail coach!" Noir yelled. "Retreat!"

Cursing under their breaths, his galloping men on their hired horses obeyed. Noir hoped they looked like a group of foolish young men out for a lark. Mail coaches—like the stagecoach they had already let fly by unmolested—were just too well defended to risk. Even if they succeeded, they would have the authorities on their tails, complicating matters.

"What matters?" Boucher had demanded.

"*All* matters," Noir had retorted. "We don't want them waiting or us at Finsborough jail."

"Then why don't we rob the coach *after* we break out our men?" Caron asked.

"I thought of that, but we'll probably need to make a speedy escape, and if we don't already have the money, our smuggling friends will leave us in England to rot."

They had seen the sense in that, although it was frustrating to have wasted two hours watching and waiting in increasing boredom, just to let two coaches and a farmer's cart go by.

However, before they could retreat to their hiding place, Noir's keen ears picked up another set of hooves approaching. As a curricle swept around the bend, drawn by a pair of matched bays, Lefevre on the other side of the road signaled that no other vehicle was following.

Noir grinned. "Ours!" he yelled, and they all closed in on the unfortunate driver, pulling scarves up over their mouths and waving pistols in the air, forcing him to stop.

At first, the very young gentleman—he could not have been twenty years old–seemed more amused than frightened, as though he really did suspect them of being his fellow, callow youths larking about. Only when he was fully surrounded and he had peered around all his captors, did his smile fade, and a frown of confusion replaced it.

"What the devil?" he demanded. "What do you fellows want?"

"Um, your money or your life," Noir stated, since he understood that to be the choice given by English highwaymen.

"You're joking me!" the young gentleman fumed.

"Sadly not," Noir said cheerfully. "Cough up, my friend!"

"No, damn it, I won't. It isn't fair, five of you ganging up on me, and I won't give you my dashed money. It's mine!"

"Robbery isn't fair," Noir pointed out. "And I don't see why you're so bad-tempered about it. We could just shoot you and take your money. At least we're giving you the choice."

The young man scowled at them. "I just won that money," he said bitterly. "I *never* win at cards. And now that I finally have, I also have the *appalling* luck to be held up on my way home! Here, Walton didn't put you up to this, did he?"

"I am not acquainted with any Walton," Noir said. He glanced at Caron and waved his pistol toward the gentleman's valise. "Come, down you get and pay your toll," he added, and the young man stepped down with ill grace.

He scowled direly at Noir as his greatcoat pockets were searched and a large wad of bank notes extracted. From his position at the horses' heads, Boucher grinned. More than enough to keep the smuggler captain on their side. So much, in fact, that it gave Noir another idea.

He glanced at the valise, which Caron had opened to reveal a few shirts and an evening coat, and then considered their victim who, by now, seemed to have recovered his temper and become resigned to his poverty. Noir rather liked that he showed no fear, only wariness.

"I'll tell you what, my friend," he said. "I'll give you this amount of money back if you swear silence about being robbed."

"Oh, no! My father's the dashed magistrate! Under no circumstances will I keep silent about you."

"Nonsense," Noir cajoled. "You're a man who likes a wager, clearly. I'll fight you for your silence."

"Boxing?" the young man asked with a hint of hope.

"No."

"Well, I don't have a pistol and even if I did, one of you would kill me."

"Nonsense. We'll fight with swords for first blood."

"Captain, for the love of—" Boucher began.

"Oh, very well," Noir said reluctantly. "We won't fight." He yanked Caron's hat off his head and threw it in the air. "If you hit the hat while it's in the air, I give you back half the money and you may blab all you like. If you don't hit it, I give you back this small handful of notes, and you swear silence."

The young man thought about it, then laughed. "Very well, but you will have to give me your pistol."

"I will. But bear in mind as you shoot that my men all have their pistols trained on you."

"If you think that will upset my aim, you're wrong," the gentleman declared.

Solemnly, they walked a little way from the curricle. Lefevre's and Boucher's weapons followed their progress. Noir handed over his pistol, gave the other man a moment to weigh it and take aim, then threw Caron's hat into the air.

The gentleman fired, and the hat fluttered to the ground. The young man strode after it and picked it up. His face fell. "Damn, I missed."

Noir extracted the pistol from his fingers and examined the hat, too. "You did. But never mind. You still have some money back, so you're better off than before your card game."

"Double or quits," the young man suggested.

Noir laughed and plonked the now grubby hat back on Caron's head. "No."

Caron was stuffing the evening coat back into the valise, shaking his head to show he'd found no more money or anything else they could use.

"Going somewhere agreeable?" Noir asked, taking the coat and holding it up. It was a fine garment.

"A neighbor's ball. The coat needs altered for me. I didn't grow as much as my father assumed I would,"

"But it would fit *me* perfectly. I'll buy it from you." Noir added another few notes to the bundle he gave back to the gentleman. "So, who goes to this ball, besides your family?"

"Everyone," the young gentleman replied. "It's at Audley Park, Lord Overton's seat, and all the world and his wife will be there."

Noir began to smile. *Now*, he had a plan.

PREPARING FOR THE ball was surprisingly light-hearted fun. Isabelle slept late and enjoyed the relaxed atmosphere of the house. She had been here many times before, and it had never felt like this. Clearly, it was Cecily's doing. She had saved Patrick, and Isabelle could almost have imagined that the house knew it.

Cecily, Jane, and Cecily's dresser, Cranston, all gathered around Isabelle's only decent evening gown, which was a diaphanous garment of a deep, pleasing shade of midnight blue. She had packed it to have something pretty to wear while dining with Sir Maurice. For that reason alone, she would have been happy never to see it again.

"It is so delicate," Cecily observed. "It would be a shame to weigh it down with masses of lace and ribbon."

"Tiny diamonds," Cranston said.

Isabelle regarded her sardonically.

"Just a few," the maid said defensively. "Just to make the gown shimmer and sparkle like a starry night."

"I didn't realize you were so poetic," Cecily said admiringly.

Cranston blushed.

"It is a lovely idea," Isabelle said. "But unfortunately, I have left my collection of tiny diamonds at home."

"I have some," Jane said unexpectedly.

"No, you don't," Isabelle disputed.

"I do! They were Mama's." With that, she sped off, presumably to her own chamber.

"If they were," Cecily observed, "I can't imagine Elvira Longstone letting her keep them, let alone escape with them."

But soon enough, the child returned with a box, inside which were, indeed, a collection of about ten glittering little stones.

"Uncle Patrick gave me them when I came to stay," she confided. "It is a secret, but I would love you to wear them, Cousin Izzy."

Isabelle picked up the box, examining the treasure within. She was no expert, but she rather thought that while some of them might be glass, the others were almost certainly real diamonds. Either way, they would have the desired effect.

"They are beautiful, and if you trust me with them, I would be honored to wear them," Isabelle said at last. She cocked her head at Cranston. "If you can manage to sew them on securely enough?"

"Cranston can do anything," Cecily assured her.

And so, it proved. Cranston not only made the dress sparkle in an entirely subtle yet eye-catching manner whenever it moved, she also came to dress Isabelle's hair for the ball, bringing with her a tiara Lady Cecily had decided would go delightfully with the ensemble.

Isabelle had to admit it was perfect for the occasion. Beautiful and yet understated as befitted a recent widow who had thoroughly disapproved of her husband. She could carry it off, and do so just for herself and her friends. Not for any man.

And if no one else was brave enough to ask her to dance, both Patrick and Lord Torbridge would. It wasn't until she actually sat in the carriage bound for Audley Park for pre-ball dinner, that she suddenly remembered the probable presence of Sir Maurice Ashton.

He had been invited. That must have been why he had agreed to their assignation being at the Hart, close to Audley Park. He hadn't mentioned that other London acquaintances, who might easily have recognized them, were liable to be traveling at the same time in the same direction. But then discretion had never been his aim.

She drew in her breath, very conscious of Jane's excited presence in the carriage, squashed between her uncle and Lord Torbridge. "Sir Maurice Ashton was at the Hart on Wednesday night, too."

"I know," Torbridge said without expression. "I spoke to him." He met her gaze, and a faint smile flickered. "Even the sternest watchers over propriety must count the sheer quantity of your chaperones on Wednesday night as superior to a mere maid."

Well, if Torbridge remained on her side, she might still brush through the evening without any slights. At any rate, however reprehensible her decision to go to the Hart, she had done nothing wrong and refused to behave as if she had.

At Audley Park, they were welcomed with genuine pleasure by Lord and Lady Overton, who were, in fact, the parents-in-law of Cecily's brother, the Duke of Alvan. Also present for dinner were two of their daughters and their husbands, Lord Dunstan and the scandalous Mr. Cromarty, heir to the old Earl of Silford. Like the rest of the family, they were lively and witty and easy to like. Besides them, there were some local gentry, including the Laceys, whom she knew slightly, and her cousin Elvira Longstone, escorted by her son Henry.

In the flurry of introductions and greetings, it was easy to be quickly civil to her cousins and pass on. And though Isabelle had once hoped to mend the rift between them, she found she was actually glad of this distance.

Looking back, they had always wanted something from her for their charity. An unpaid companion and housekeeper, an equally unpaid governess. And then, despite knowing her innocence, they had dropped her as soon as the scandal of Pierre de Renarde was public.

They had supplied an occasional place to stay, even a purpose in life in allowing her to teach Jane, but it had never been her home.

Even her house with Pierre had never been home. Not after he had brought his first mistress there.

*Come with me. Come home.*

She blinked away the memory yet again.

Among the London guests was, as she'd suspected, Sir Maurice Ashton. She was glad to discover there was no need to initiate distance between them, since his greeting was only barely civil. Unfortunately, she was placed beside him for dinner, but at least Torbridge was on the other side, so she barely needed to converse with Ashton at all.

THE BALL WAS a lavish affair, the first the Overtons had held since their return from abroad a year or so ago. The rumor was, they had been flat broke until their least marriageable daughter had somehow caught the Duke of Alvan, the country's most eligible bachelor, in matrimony. If that was true, Lady Overton was certainly enjoying the opportunity to splash out now. The ballroom was decorated with greenery and what seemed like miles of draped silk. It was lit by hundreds of candles, which Isabelle couldn't help hoping were secure enough not fall into the silk at the first draught.

She danced the first enjoyable country set with Lord Torbridge, realizing how much she had missed such activity in recent months. After that, she stood in front of the French window in conversation with some amusing people she knew only vaguely.

"Madame de Renarde," said an oddly familiar male voice beside her, and she turned, smiling in polite greeting.

"Lieutenant Steele," she exclaimed, offering her hand at once. "What an unexpected pleasure to find you here." As he bowed over her hand, she took in his arm, now resting in a heroic sling tied across his good shoulder. "I hope you are well enough."

He wrinkled his nose at the sling. "You mean this abomination? The local physician insisted I wear it to keep from pulling the wound. I feel like a fraud because I'm sure it's on the mend. Even the doctor said so."

"Best do as he says, Lieutenant. No point in consulting him otherwise."

"I wouldn't have bothered. It was Mrs. Villin who brought him. But there, I don't mean to sound ungracious! I trust you are none the worse for our adventure?"

"Of course not. You must know I have no sensibility."

"I don't believe that. You merely hold yourself together well. I, for one, give you the credit for getting us all out of the fix alive, though I'll not deny I didn't like it at the time."

She regarded him uneasily. "I hope you haven't said so to anyone else."

"Of course not."

"And are you still at the Hart?" she asked hastily, distracting him from the affront to his tact.

"I am. I only meant to stay the one night and travel on to visit my parents, but the doctor was not keen on my riding just yet. I expect I shall leave it until Sunday or Monday. What of you, madame? Did you not mean to return to London?"

"I did, but I called on my old friends the Vernes, and they persuaded me to stay. And Lady Overton was kind enough to invite me tonight. Are you a friend of Lord Overton? Or Mr. Cromarty, perhaps?"

"Not exactly," Steele replied with a faint smile. "After you left the Hart, there was a positive invasion of people, desperate to hear all about our adventure. Lord Overton was among them and seemed to regard me as some kind of hero because I fought Captain le Noir. Even though I came off worst."

"Don't feel badly. He was wounded, too."

"Hmm," Steele said doubtfully. "In any case, his lordship invited me tonight and kindly introduced me to his wife and family and so many lords and ladies, I confess I am quite overwhelmed."

"Make the most of your heroic status," Isabelle advised. "Tomorrow, it is liable to be someone else."

"So beautiful, yet so cynical," mourned another man suddenly appearing between them in a draught of icy air to press a glass of champagne into each of their hands.

Bemused, Isabelle stared up at the speaker and the glass slipped from her suddenly numb fingers.

*Captain le Noir.*

# CHAPTER NINE

CAPTAIN LE NOIR—WHO must have entered through the window, hence the draught—deftly caught the falling glass and presented it once more. She grasped it blindly, her heart seeming to plummet into her stomach. The sight of him was so totally unexpected, so appalling, that it must have been hysteria prompting her to laugh.

"Oh, dear God," she said shakily.

He was dressed in black evening clothes that fitted his tall, lean frame almost perfectly, his cravat neatly tied. A smile lurked on his lips and in his eyes as they met hers, clearly enjoying her reaction. He looked ridiculously handsome.

"Are you insane?" Steele demanded furiously. "Did we just lie to our countrymen for nothing?"

"Hush, sir, no one lied," Noir said, reaching behind him from another glass, which he raised in a toast. "To freedom. And beautiful eyes." He took a sip and seemed pleased. "I think this must be smuggled, too."

"What the devil are you doing here?" Isabelle demanded, finally recovering her voice.

"There was no time for a proper farewell when I left, so I thought I would come here to pay my respects and thanks and wish you *adieu*."

Despite the excitement she couldn't prevent, a chill passed down Isabelle's spine. "Dear God, you have not brought your men here to raid?"

"Of course not," he said, startled. "How stupid do you think I am?"

"Very!" Isabelle and Steele said together, and he laughed.

"Nonsense. I shall merely drink a glass of champagne with you both and then vanish as discreetly as I arrived."

"Captain, you are putting us in an impossible situation," Steele said between his teeth. "I have no choice but to arrest you."

"You have no weapon," Noir pointed out. He smiled. "I do."

"Are you threatening us?" Isabelle demanded.

His eyebrows flew up. "Lord, no. The boot was on the other foot, but look, here is Sir Maurice come to join our reunion."

Sir Maurice, certainly, was walking in their direction with a couple of male acquaintances, but his covert attention did not appear to be on Noir but on Isabelle. Perhaps he had decided to forgive her. Perhaps he had boasted too much to his friends and had to prove her compliance. And none of that mattered, she thought in panic as his gaze shifted to take in his competition—Steele…and Noir.

His eyes widened at the impossibility. And then, in outrage, he left his companions far behind as he stormed toward them, his mouth already open to shout the alarm that would send everyone in the ballroom into a panicked spin.

Hastily, Isabelle seized Noir's right arm, to stop him drawing his weapon, whether sword or pistol.

But with great aplomb, Lieutenant Steele stepped up to the situation once more, hastily striding in front of Sir Maurice, seizing *his* arm in an apparently friendly but quite iron grasp and twitching him in the other direction.

Between his smiling teeth, Isabelle was sure he said, "Not the way, sir. We'd just lose him in the panic."

"You have to go," Isabelle said urgently.

"How can I when you hold my arm so tightly?"

At once, she tried to release him, but he clamped her hand between his arm and his body.

"Why are you here?" she asked helplessly, giving in.

"To drink champagne with you." He began to stroll around the edges of the busy dance floor and for the benefit of any onlookers, she smiled and sipped her champagne.

"Liar," she said.

"I wanted to see you. I don't mind what we do."

"Captain—"

"Call me Armand," he interrupted.

"Why?" she demanded starkly.

His eyebrows flew up. "It's my name."

A surprised choke of laughter escaped her. "I mean, as you very well know, there is no point in calling you anything at all! You will be arrested this time. There is no way out of it."

"There is usually a way out," he said vaguely. "That is, there always has been."

"But no guns this time," she pleaded. "No swords. There are children in the house."

"Of course. Who brings weapons to a party?"

She frowned. "You just said *you* did."

"I lied to keep Steele busy."

Again, she wanted to laugh, but her anxious eyes caught sight of Steele and Ashton and the notion died at birth. They were talking to Lord Torbridge and Overton's son-in-law, Sydney Cromarty, who were watching her and Noir. An instant later, they moved in different directions. So did Steele, toward Lord Overton, while Sir Maurice strode toward Lord Dunstan.

"Where are your men?" she demanded.

"I left them behind."

Isabelle didn't know whether to hit him or simply be grateful. "They are gathering to arrest you," she said abruptly. "You will be overwhelmed by sheer numbers."

"I will," he agreed. "But not yet."

She stared at him. "I don't understand why you've come here! You should be safely back in France by now. Or at least as safe as someone like you could ever be. Instead, you walk straight into the lion's den."

"Are you concerned for me?" he asked lightly, although his eyes devoured her.

She wrenched her gaze free. "Yes," she muttered. "And for me, since you have singled me out and distinguished me with your attentions. Just as I was reviving my reputation."

"Look as disapproving as you like. Try to draw free again. Don't worry, I won't let you."

She glared at him once more. "That is *not* my chief anxiety!"

The dance had ended, and couples were milling off the floor. Among them, moving inexorably in Noir's direction, were several solitary, purposeful men. And only yards away, young Matthew Lacey, his eyes almost goggling as he stared open-mouthed at Armand. The Frenchman inclined his head and smiled, raising his glass to Matthew before setting it down on a table.

"You know each other," Isabelle blurted. "How on earth do you know Matthew?"

"I'm wearing his coat, but don't tell anyone."

Matthew, too, began to stride toward them.

"To the window," she urged, tugging Armand's arm in panic. "It's your only chance."

"Someone is there," he said without obvious concern.

"Captain—"

"Armand," he reminded her.

"Armand, you will be taken!" she said, no longer bothering to hide her distress. "Arrested and imprisoned. Does that not matter to you?"

"No," he said, "for it won't happen until I've danced with you." And without warning, as the orchestra struck up once more, he swept her between Lord Dunstan and Matthew Lacey and onto the dance floor, where other couples were gathering. Men on their own were out of place there, and some of his would be-captors were forced to move off the dance floor, away from them.

Armand's arm came hard around her waist, and she found herself gliding into the waltz. She fought it, but there was no denying it felt so good, so tempting, to be so close to him, to dance as if they were friends...lovers.

His thumb caressed her hand. He waltzed as she had known he would, graceful yet somehow untamed, holding her a shade too close as he swept her around the floor.

"You really ask me to believe this is all to dance with me?" she demanded, desperately trying to fight her body's surrender.

"Is it so hard to accept?"

"Yes! Armand, you could die for this." She held his gaze in sudden terror. "Please tell me you are not trying to die."

"I am not trying to die." His voice, suddenly, was hoarse. "I just wanted to see you one more time."

"Why?" she asked despairingly.

"To learn about you as there was no opportunity to do at the inn. To know what your life is like, how you grew up, your wishes and dreams, your loves and hates."

"That is a tall order for one dance with a ring of men trying not to stare too hard at us."

"Ignore them. When did you leave France?"

"When I was three years old, after the revolutionaries captured and killed my uncle and cousins."

"How did you escape?"

"I don't remember."

"Yes, you do," he said softly.

She shook her head. "No. I just remember...being afraid, hiding in a dark, cold spaces under floorboards, under the seats of smelly carriages. And a ship full of scary men. And then rain and squalid rooms before our English cousins found us. After that, it was better.

We lived in a comfortable, warm house, with enough to eat." Somehow, under that intense, steady gaze, the words continued to spill out. She told him about her parents' deaths in the same month, when she was ten years old, how she had enjoyed growing more important to the Longstones, becoming their de facto housekeeper by the time she was fourteen years old. And then had come the trip to London, where she had met Pierre, a fellow émigré.

"No one knew what I saw in him. He was handsome in a way, and he had cleverly made money in the city, but no one would have called him dashing. But he pursued me most flatteringly, and I... I knew there was more to him, and I wanted to know that man. I convinced myself I was in love with him, and I married him."

"You told me he was a...bounder," he observed, loosely translating the less than ladylike term she had used at the Hart.

"It took me less than a week of marriage to discover it. He took my pride and my self-respect, but for two years I was a good wife to him, giving him freedom, turning a blind eye, keeping his home, which was never mine. In that time, I learned to grow a hard shell, to play the sophisticate who cared little where her husband strayed. And then one day, I realized I *really* didn't care where he was, or even if I never saw him again."

His expression was attentive, but revealed neither pity nor contempt. "So, what did you do?"

"I left him and returned to my cousins in Sussex. And there I met another man I thought I loved."

"Did you?"

"Perhaps." She met his gaze boldly. "We formed a liaison which kept us both sane in difficult times. We never pried beneath each other's...veils, but I believed we understood each other. I stood with him through a terrible tragedy. And then it was over."

"How?"

She smiled faintly. "I think we just grew apart. It was no longer our time. I varied my time between London—when Pierre was not there—and Sussex. I became governess to my cousin's granddaughter, and my one and only lover married another. Just before Pierre died a traitor to the country that had harbored us both."

She danced backward and turned with him, surely even closer than before. "Now it is your turn," she said breathlessly. "Who knows what those watching will imagine I've been telling you. Thank God I know no government secrets."

"What do you want to know?"

"About your life. Your wife."

"You won't like my life."

"You won't know that until you tell me."

"I don't even have a name. I don't know where I was born. Somewhere euphemistically referred to as the Paris streets, but probably a brothel or an orphanage. Certainly, I grew up in such places until I was eight or nine, when a defrocked priest discovered me trying to teach myself to read and count between bouts of thieving. It was he who gave me the surname le Noir, because, he said, my hair was blacker than my heart. Before that, I had just been Armand, though I've no idea who first called me that. Anyway, he took me in, sent me to school. Sometimes I went, sometimes I ran away. But somehow, I got a smattering of education, enough to join the army, where they made me a junior officer."

"Were you a good soldier?"

"Oh, yes. And somehow between campaigns, I met Rose. We married, had a son, and they followed the drum with me. I thought my life was complete, happy. And when the war was over, we were going to buy a farm in the south, where her people lived… And then a fever swept through the ranks, and both Rose and Robert were gone. Along with my life. And so, I sought out distractions. Not to kill myself as people think. Just to *stop* myself dying." An almost apologetic smile flickered across his lips. "Do you understand?"

Stricken, she stared at him. "I think I do," she whispered.

He swallowed. "So much for our pasts. What of the future?"

She shrugged, almost impatient now. "Who knows? I shall be a governess if I can and see where that leads me. What of you?"

"I will have that farm one day, when the war ends. I shall grow grapes and figs and make wine. And I would like to dance with you."

She let that lie in silence. It was as if a bubble had formed around them, separating them from the other dancers, from the Englishmen waiting to arrest him. They only had this dance. There could be no others.

Or could there?

"In the old days, you would never have been an officer," she blurted. "Is that why you love your Bonaparte?"

"It's one reason I appreciate him, I don't love him. He is simply the best soldier in Europe and saved both France and the revolution...before he betrayed it."

"By crowning himself emperor, you mean?"

"Why get rid of one monarch just to replace him with another? Even if he is rather more given to sense and equality. He should never have done it. Now, no one disagrees with him or they lose their place. He grows into tyranny, listening to no one and believing in his own invincibility. And so, we have the Russian campaign."

"Do many in France think as you?"

He blinked his eyes back into focus. "Do you want information to give your adopted government?"

"No, I was wondering if the French might end the war themselves by getting rid of Bonaparte."

He smiled. "What would you do then?"

"I don't know." From the corner of her eye, she saw Torbridge speaking to Verne, gazing between the dancers toward her and Armand. Worse, the music, clearly, was coming to an end. Their dance was over. "It doesn't matter," she said in despair.

His fingers tightened on hers. "It's all that matters. Pull free of me as though you hate me."

"I do hate you," she whispered, yanking her hand free at the last note.

Armand smiled. "Excellent." He released her and bowed, walking swiftly through the crowd of dancers, not to the window but to the entrance to the ballroom.

From their suddenly panicked movements, both Torbridge and Verne had lost him. She walked toward them, instinctively drawing their attention so they would not see Armand. *What in God's name am I doing? He is an enemy. My enemy!*

*Not mine, not mine...*

Torbridge started toward her, then was suddenly distracted and veered toward the door. Isabelle followed because there was nothing else she could do.

A few moments later, the crowd parted, and she caught sight of Armand's back, suddenly lunging forward and rushing out of the ballroom with several gentlemen on his tail, trying not to look as if they were running.

A few people glanced around in amusement, but most went on their way without even noticing.

By the time Isabelle got to the top of the ballroom steps, several men were pounding down the passage, gathering up servants as they went and calling to each other. After a quick glance behind her, Isabelle picked up her skirts and ran after them.

At the far end, the passage widened into a broad landing. Armand's pursuers were leaping down the staircase after him. And they were catching up—until Armand suddenly threw himself on the curved, highly polished bannister and sped down it with a blatant cry of triumph.

At the bottom, he jumped, landing on his feet which seemed already to be running. Isabelle almost laughed, for it really looked as if he was going to make the front door and freedom.

Until he ran straight into two very large footmen rushing from either end of the entrance hall, and they all landed on the floor in an untidy pile.

When they finally wrestled him to his feet, he had a footman hanging onto each arm and Captain Cromarty, Lord Overton's son-in-law, held a pistol aimed at his heart.

"My good man," Armand said breathlessly to Cromarty. "Who the devil takes a weapon to a party?"

This time Isabelle really did laugh, although she was obliged to turn away before it turned into tears.

# CHAPTER TEN

A RMAND LE NOIR didn't mind a little rough handling as they dragged him across the hall and shoved him into some kind of office. When they slammed and locked the door, the darkness appeared to be absolute.

Picking himself off the floor, he waited for his eyes to grow accustomed to the gloom, but apart from the faint line of light visible under the door, he couldn't see a damned thing. He felt along the wall, bumping into something that turned out to be a bookcase. Trailing his fingers over it, he found his way back to the wall, the corner, and the window. The shutters were fastened. There was no time to do more, for the two footmen entered again. One glared at him while the other lit two lamps. Another man walked in, and the footmen left.

The man was a gentleman, perfectly dressed and groomed—one of those who'd been chasing him. His expression was mild, unthreatening. But his eyes were sharp.

"Please, sit down," this gentleman invited, indicating the chair at the desk in front of the window.

Obligingly, Noir sat.

The gentleman sat opposite and folded his arms across the desk, "Do I gather I am addressing Captain le Noir?"

"You are."

"I'm Torbridge, a friend of the Overtons—your hosts—and a frequent patron, you might say, of the Hart Inn."

"Very comfortable place," Noir allowed. "Interesting man, Villin."

"You're quite an interesting man yourself, Captain."

"Really?" Noir eased his shoulder where the footmen had almost yanked his arm out of his socket. He hoped it hadn't made his wound bleed again, because he hadn't had time to have it stitched. "In what way?"

"You didn't kill Lieutenant Steele, though you could have. I'm fairly sure you made some kind of pact with the Villins and their guests that let you escape while leaving behind the prisoners you came for."

"I don't know what you're talking about."

"Surely your English is not failing you at this stage?"

Noir, who had contemplated playing the uncomprehending foreigner, only grinned. He decided to be enigmatic instead. "What stage are we at?"

"The one where we tell the truth," Torbridge said mildly. "Why did you come back?"

"I left the Hart in a rush. I did not properly say goodbye to Mr. Steele or Sir Maurice, or even Madame de Renarde."

"But how did you know how to find them?"

"The ball at Audley Park on Friday was a frequent topic of conversation at the inn."

"Was it?"

Noir smiled winningly. "And the occupants of the coach I held up gave me directions."

Torbridge blinked, but otherwise, he was very good at hiding his expression. Which was interesting. "The coach you held up," he repeated.

It was clear the young man from the curricle had kept his word and his silence, even after recognizing him here. Armand was happy to cover that silence with his own.

He held out his arms and removed a speck of dust from his sleeve. "Where else do you imagine I would have found these impeccable clothes? Besides, I had to bribe the smuggler to put me ashore again. He was very eager to get to France, and the detour is costing me a lot of money."

For now at least, Torbridge let the matter of the robbed coach go. "That is my problem, Captain. I can't think why you are less eager to be in France."

Noir sighed. "Can't you? I suppose you are English."

Torbridge withstood the taunt without obvious difficulty. "By which you mean...?"

"The English are not known for affairs of the heart, so I am not sure you will understand."

Torbridge's lips twitch. "You ask me to believe you came back for a girl?"

"Not just any girl. Petite and dark and pretty as a picture, yet with some sense of mystery I cannot explain. The Villins don't know what they have in that girl."

For some reason, color seeped into Torbridge's face. It seemed Noir had made him angry at last. His next words, however, were calm enough. "Why do I not believe a word of that? To be frank, Captain, I believe you came back because you don't really want to go home. I think you are discontented with your lot and disapproving of your government."

"If that was true," Noir said, "there is nothing either of us can do about that."

"Perhaps there is. This war has gone on too long, too costly in lives and just about everything else. What if you and I could help put a stop to it?"

"A truce has been arranged," Noir mocked, "between the French-man Noir and the Englishman Torbridge. We expect everyone in Europe to abide by it."

Torbridge's smile didn't reach his eyes. "It is possible I speak as more than the Englishman Torbridge."

"Do you?" Noir asked with interest.

"That needn't concern you. This business is between you and me."

"What business?"

"I'll be frank, Captain, I have heard of you. Your exploits are not unknown in the Peninsula, and I have spoken to people in Germany and Italy. You are an asset to your country. A rogue asset who could help his country further by paving the way to peace."

"With good intentions?" Noir asked flippantly. "Like hell?"

"No," Torbridge replied. "With information."

Noir met his gaze. "You want me to betray my country. I wonder what I ever said or did to give anyone the idea that I would do such a thing?"

"France under Bonaparte has lost its way."

"So, I should do my best to hand it to you, who would put a Bourbon king back there instead? Thank you, I will keep my emperor and my honor."

Torbridge held his gaze. "And yet you came back."

"I did. But I can't be bought."

"Not with money," Torbridge agreed.

Noir sat back, thoroughly intrigued. "What else do you have?"

INEVITABLY, IN SPITE of the discretion employed in the ballroom, word of the Frenchman's capture began to circulate around the ballroom.

"The same man who escaped from the Hart?" Mrs. Cromarty said to her husband. "But why on earth would he come here? He is not after *you*, is he?"

Captain Cromarty looked amused. "He has no reason to be after me. I've never met him in my life."

"Why *do* you carry pistols to a party, Captain?" Isabelle asked lightly. He, too, had been involved in the search for Verne the night Pierre had died—another man who was more than he seemed. Apparently, he had been brought up to be a city banker, but to Isabelle, he seemed more of a buccaneer.

He laughed. "Old habits die hard. But I confess, I didn't bring it. It's Lord Overton's. I merely took it out of the drawer in his study. It wasn't even loaded."

"Where is he now?" Isabelle asked, trying not to sound too desperate to know. She didn't even know why she asked. There was nothing she could do for Armand now. Nothing she *would* do. And yet that felt like betrayal, too. A hard knot of discomfort, of fear, gathered in her stomach.

"Locked up in the steward's room downstairs," Cromarty replied. "Until the authorities come to take him away."

"I caught the maids peering at him through the keyhole," his wife said. "They seemed disappointed he wasn't more horrific."

"Being French," Isabelle murmured.

Mrs. Cromarty gave her a mischievous smile. "Presumably. But he seemed quite personable to me."

Isabelle drifted away. For the first time, she understood Armand's desperate search for distraction. She couldn't think about this. There was nothing she could do. And yet she didn't want him hauled off to prison.

Something caught at her mind, some connection that tugged and then vanished, leaving her frustrated but none the wiser. She kept imagining the tramp of soldiers or constables through the hall, come to take him away.

He should never have come here. Never. One dance was not enough to risk imprisonment, death. And yet she had enjoyed it. Precious moments that seemed obscene now because he was captured.

Somehow, she smiled, made conversation, watched the dancers without really seeing them. At one point, she came across Matthew

Lacey by himself, leaning against a pillar, deep in frowning thought.

"Mr. Lacey," she greeted him.

He snapped to attention and bowed. "Madame! How do you do?"

"A little baffled by all the excitement, as it seems are you. How is it you know our prisoner?"

"I don't," Matthew said at once, although a slightly hunted look entered his eyes. "Never seen him before in my life. Might I fetch you some refreshment, madame?"

Intrigued, Isabelle almost attached herself to him to dig out the truth. But the boy looked so anxious and so desperate to hide the fact that she took pity on him. "I thank you, but no. You will tell me, though, if you are in trouble?"

"No trouble to get into around here," he insisted, then, presumably remembering the ordeal at the Hart, he blushed and shifted uncomfortably on his feet.

Isabelle laughed, and left him.

Almost immediately, Lord Torbridge materialized by her side. "Would you care to dance, Madame? Or just take a turn around the ballroom, perhaps?"

Since talking was easier in the latter than in some country dance, she chose to walk with him, her fingers delicately on his immaculate coat.

"What will happen to him?" she asked abruptly.

And of course, Torbridge knew exactly whom she meant. "Interesting question. The answer is, I don't yet know."

She blinked. "I thought you would say, prison, even execution."

"It's true he is a dangerous man," Torbridge allowed. "And dangerous to our country's war efforts. But it does seem a shame that a man of such obvious talents should simply...go away, one way or another."

She searched his eyes, afraid to hope. "I'm not sure I follow you. Have you...have you let him go?"

"Of course not," he said, apparently shocked, though Isabelle could have sworn he wasn't in the slightest. "Though it's interesting you bring up the idea. I would very much like to let him go…if he made an undertaking to work for us."

"He won't. He is, literally, a child of the revolution."

"I talked to him," Torbridge said, by way of agreement. "He was interested in what I had to say. But he was not even tempted."

Her heart ached. "Then is that not the end of the matter?"

He shook his head. "No, for there has to be a reason he came ashore again. There has to be a reason he came here to Audley Park this evening."

She gazed at him, avidly waiting for him to reach a conclusion.

His lips quirked. "You, madame. I think the reason is you."

Emotion surged, boiling, clashing with the sudden snap of fear. She too walked a tightrope here.

"Do I have to defend myself still from such accusations?" she managed. "I thought you of all people understood that I was never part of my husband's actions. Of *any* of his life. I have never betrayed this country that took me in when my own would have killed me for the crime of existing. I never *will* betray it."

"I know that." He sounded surprised, genuinely apologetic. "Forgive me, I never meant to imply otherwise. Nor do I wish to be indelicate, but it is nonetheless true that attraction can often be inconvenient."

With an effort, she continued to meet his gaze in silence.

He smiled faintly. "It was noticed in the Hart by several people. He liked you. It was you who talked him into leaving the prisoners and avoiding a costly pitched battle with Brandon's men. In short, he listens to you, and it's my belief he risked coming here for you. At the back of his mind, somewhere, he wants to stay here with you."

Blood seeped into her face. "But he won't."

"There are options. The man undoubtedly has information that could help us. He could spend the rest of the war in a relatively comfortable prison, simply talking to us. He would be able to read, write, receive visitors, even go on excursions under parole."

"He won't," Isabelle said again.

Torbridge went on as though she had not spoken. "Or, he could go home as our agent. Oh, not to help us win the war as such. I know he won't do that. But to help bring about peace. To remove Bonaparte. I have reason to believe the French people are tired of constant war. He could help bring it about without betraying a single French life."

A frown flickered across her face. "Did he agree to that?"

"No." Torbridge paused by the table near the window, where Armand had appeared only an hour ago. He picked up a glass of champagne and gave it to her with a slight bow. "However, I am not you."

Her stomach twisted. "What do you mean?"

"I mean, it makes a difference who asks." He picked up a glass of his own and raised it to her. "You would be doing your country a great service.

AND SO, FIVE minutes later, one of the large footmen who had finally caught Armand, crouched down and peered through the office keyhole before straightening, unlocking the door, and standing aside for her.

"We'll be right out here, ma'am," he said darkly. "Just shout if he gives you any trouble at all. Even if he looks at you the wrong way."

"Thank you," Isabelle managed and walked into the room. Her heart pounded.

Armand, sitting behind the desk, sprang to his feet. His black hair was tousled, and a bruise had formed at the side of his face. She came to a halt in the middle of the room as the door closed behind her.

Desperately, she tried to squash the insistent voice in her mind whispering that this was possible, that happiness could be hers, a happiness she had never even hoped for in ten years. *This man, this man...*

"Isabelle." A tender smile flickered across his face. He came out from behind the desk, walking inexorably toward her.

Her mouth went dry. Something very like panic hit her, and yet she let him take her in his arms. She even raised her face to his, and when he kissed her, her eyes closed of their own accord. She threw her hand up to his rough, warm cheek, just to bring him closer. Her mouth opened wide to his passion, matching his hunger as she kissed him back.

And then, with a sob that was only half-laughter, she murmured against his lips. "They watch through the keyhole."

He drew back reluctantly, dragging one chair back from the desk and out of view from the door. She sat and watched him bring the other from behind the desk.

"How did you get in?" he murmured, sitting and reaching for her hand.

"Torbridge sent me," she said frankly.

His smile was rueful. "That man sees too much. Who the devil is he?"

"I think he does some kind of work for the government, but he doesn't like people to know."

"He reminds me of someone, though I can't put my finger on why."

"Who?" she asked, distracted.

"The defrocked priest who educated me. Why did he send you?"

"He thought I could persuade you to stay in England. Or return to France on his agenda."

His smile was lopsided. "Don't try. You can tempt me, but you can't persuade me."

She looked him in the eyes. *"Come with me,"* she quoted. "Why did you ask me that?"

"Impulse. You are not happy here. It struck me that I could make you happy in France. That we could make each other happy."

She clung to his fingers. "And is that really why you came back? Why you came here tonight?"

He hesitated. "Out of many possible courses, it's the one I chose. I thought of climbing through your bedchamber window, but it seemed a trifle presumptuous."

Laughter caught in her throat. "Still, I would not put it past you. Armand, do I delude myself? Do you think we have the beginnings here of…of something more?"

"Of love?" he said steadily. "Perhaps. If we meet again."

"Can we not make that happen? Help bring peace through our connection?"

The tender smile faded from his eyes. "Are you his bribe?"

She closed her eyes and nodded. "Am I not enough?"

"Oh, my sweet, if I thought you meant it…"

She whipped her hand away, her eyes flying open to glare at him. "Of course I mean it! What do you take me for? Dear God, I do not even know if you have a new wife! Mistresses and children scattered across France—across Europe! I try to give us this chance, and you throw contempt in my face!"

"Isabelle!" He leaned forward, seizing not her hands this time, but her face, holding it between his palms. "No deals. No Torbridge. Just come home with me."

Angrily, she tried to tug his hands away and ended by clinging to them. "Armand, that will be after the war."

"Will you wait?"

"Will you?"

"I'm beginning to think I would wait a lifetime for you. That I already have."

In pain, she kissed his palm. "They'll put you in prison. I don't think Torbridge will let them execute you. For some reason, you are too valuable to him."

"Will you visit me?"

"You know I will."

"And you'll ask me for nothing?"

"I might ask, but I know you won't tell."

One of his hands moved, clasping hers and carrying it to his lips. "One day…" He smiled. "I'm glad I came."

"So am I, and yet I wish you had not. I wish you were safe in France."

"Safe," he said disparagingly. "There are many more distractions here. How long do we have?"

"Until the soldiers come for you." She smiled unhappily. "Again."

"Don't be here when they do. Say goodbye now."

She leaned into him, meeting his lips. She tasted the salt of her own tears, and then a knock sounded on the door and they sprang apart.

Isabelle jumped to her feet, dashing the back of her hand across her eyes. "I'm coming," she called and walked out of the room without looking back.

Torbridge was waiting for her. Whatever she said now would feel like betrayal of someone or something, so she fell back on what she had always been taught. The truth.

"If you let him go, he will give you nothing. You might learn something from keeping him here and visiting him in prison, but I doubt it will be what you want."

Torbridge nodded as though he wasn't surprised. "It will be something," he said. "Thank you, madame. I know this wasn't easy for you."

"You will see he is treated well?"

"I will."

"Thank you. Excuse me." She hurried away to the ladies' cloak-room.

There, since she was alone, it would have been easy to give in to the rare bout of weeping still threatening in her throat. But she didn't. It would help no one. So, she merely splashed water on her face and repinned Cecily's tiara. Then, with her head held high, she returned to the ballroom in search of distraction, for he was right. She did not wish to see the soldiers, the constables, or whoever came to take him away.

*Take him where?*

Impulsively, she looked around the ballroom for Torbridge, but he was dancing. She moved among the throng until she came across Lord Overton and Mr. Lacey who was, in fact, a local magistrate.

"Tell me," she said after their civil greeting, "where will they take Captain le Noir?"

"For tonight? Just to Finsborough jail," Lacey replied.

Finsborough jail, where the escaped French prisoners were also kept.

*Out of many possible courses, it's the one I chose…*

*Where are your men?* she had asked him.

*I left them behind.* He did not say where.

*Dear God, you have not brought your men here to raid?* she had asked when he had first appeared beside her and Steele.

*Of course not. How stupid do you think I am?* Because they were not raiding Audley Park. Of course they were not. Not when the prisoners were…

She found she was staring at Overton. "Finsborough jail. That's where he wants to be!"

They blinked at her, then looked uncomfortably at each other.

"Don't you see?" she said urgently. "He hasn't given up. He never gives up! He's still trying to rescue the prisoners!"

Overton closed his mouth. Lacey charged toward the ballroom entrance, Overton and Isabelle on his heels.

"Open the damned door!" Overton yelled, and the large footman charged across the entrance hall to obey.

As he flung the door wide, Isabelle's heart plummeted.

The room was empty.

It was as if he had vanished into thin air.

# CHAPTER ELEVEN

"**H**OW THE DEVIL…?" Overton strode behind the desk to the window and threw open the window shutters. They weren't fastened. They had only been closed over. Like the window. "The window was locked! All the damned windows on the ground floor were locked this afternoon—against any opportunistic thieves, you understand."

He and Lacey peered at the window, scowling at it, while Isabelle leaned against the wall, watching them.

"It's been forced," Lacey said grimly. "The lock is broken."

"He had no tools to do that!" Overton objected. "We searched him, and there can't have been anything in here. For God's sake, however he managed it, would Gerard out there not have heard something? Most of the staff have spent every spare second peering through the dashed keyhole!"

"He must have done it earlier," Isabelle said numbly. "Before he revealed himself to the lieutenant and me. I'm sorry. It made sense to me that he would persuade you to put him inside the jail."

"Perhaps you're not so far wrong," Lacey said grimly. "Perhaps this is merely a detour. My lord, I hate to spoil your party, but let's get together as many young men as possible and ride at once to Finsborough!"

ALTHOUGH ISABELLE FELT far too restless, her nerves far too frayed, to simply continue at the ball, there wasn't much else she could do. She had no excuse to go to Finsborough with the men. But some other idea, still elusive, was pulling at her mind and vanishing before she could catch it.

*Distraction*, she remembered. And so, she donned her sociable face, as she had done so often in the past, ever since she had had to preserve her pride from Pierre's very public neglect. No one had known in those days that inside the bright, seductive shell, she had shrunk like a kicked dog. And no one should know now that her heart had left with the Frenchman, how desperately afraid she was that she would be responsible for his capture or even his death. Even his escape would be bad because...because... Damn, she should know. Why couldn't she think?

It was while she waltzed with Sir Maurice, that it came to her.

"You really are the most stunning creature," he said, as though the words were wrung from him. In fact, for the first time, she noticed a rather dazzled look about his eyes.

"I hope my effect is not so severe."

"Too late. Tell me, madame, may we not put the unpleasantness at the Hart behind us and begin again?"

"Begin what again?" she asked bluntly.

"Madame, I am at your feet."

"No, you're not. And truly, I never wanted a man at my feet. Certainly not one who has broken all trust by bandying a lady's name about a public taproom."

He flushed. "I never mentioned your name."

"But you made it clear enough who you meant. You may be sure I was recognized on the strength of your not naming me. This will be our last dance, Sir Maurice. From now on, we may be civil acquaintances and discuss as many witty nothings as you like. But we will never be friends."

He was too flabbergasted to do more than stutter, which pleased her vaguely before the turn of the dance brought young Matthew Lacey into her view. Despite his determination not to speak to her of Armand, he was one of those who had ridden off with Lacey and Torbridge for Finsborough.

"What is he doing back?" she wondered aloud, for it was far too soon for them to have made it to the jail and back, even without stopping.

"They probably met the men coming *from* Finsborough to take Noir into custody."

She gazed at him blindly while everything dropped into place. Finally.

He hadn't come here to see her on his way to Finsborough. He had come to be arrested, to bring him to Audley Park to collect those men who would otherwise be guarding their French prisoners. While Noir's men, taking advantage of the guards' absence, would break their countrymen out.

She stopped dancing. "Let's go and find out," she said, and there was little he could do but escort her across the floor to young Mr. Lacey.

"Not needed, after all?" Sir Maurice drawled.

Matthew Lacey shrugged. "No, there were loads of men from Finsborough, including Brandon and his soldiers, so only the *really* curious carried on!"

Isabelle thought he was relieved not to be in pursuit any longer, to be free, perhaps, of some conflict of loyalty. She could understand that only too well. "Then the Finsborough men just turned around and went back with your father?" Isabelle asked.

"And Torbridge," Matthew said. He frowned at her. "Are you quite well, madame."

"No. No, I think everything has finally caught up with me," she said vaguely. *Too late. They will be too late.* "Excuse me, I think I must just find Lady Verne…"

Cecily saw her coming and immediately left her own court of admirers to meet her. "Isabelle, what is it? Are you ill?"

"I wonder… I wonder if you would mind my going home early? I would send the carriage back for you, of course."

With her innate understanding, Cecily asked no more, except to wonder if she should not have company.

"To be honest, I would rather be alone," Isabelle said. "I feel quite…overwhelmed."

"Go then, fetch your things while I have them summon the carriage."

"Thank you, Cecily. I'll explain later." *Maybe. One day.*

Ten minutes later, without fuss or escort, she walked toward the Vernes' carriage with relief. The front terrace and the drive were brightly lit, but inside the carriage would be blessed solitude and darkness.

The coachman let down the steps and held the door for her. With her foot on the first step, she paused. "Directly south of here, there is a cove, is there not? East of the one by the Hart Inn."

"Azell Cove?" the coachman asked.

"Yes, that's it. Would you mind going back to Finmarsh House via Azell Cove and the coast road?"

"It isn't exactly on the way, but I don't mind."

"Thank you," Isabelle said and climbed in.

She huddled inside her cloak and dragged the blanket over her knees. She couldn't prevent them leaving, but it might be some satisfaction to know that she'd been right about where they were leaving from.

The coach had bumped and rumbled for about ten minutes before she realized she was staring at a dark corner of the coach where there was often a pocket to be found containing a pistol with which to confront would-be highway robbers.

On impulse, she leaned forward and delved inside. Her fingers closed around something cold and metallic and pulled it out. An old but serviceable pistol.

And it was loaded.

Perhaps she could stop them after all.

THE CARRIAGE SLOWED and stopped, and Isabelle opened the window to stick her head out. The coachman looked down at her.

"Can't take the carriage any farther, ma'am. After this, the road is no more than a footpath. I'd never be able to turn the horses to come back."

"Can you turn them here?"

"That I can."

She opened the door and jumped down, the pistol hidden in her cloak. "Good. Then, I'll just walk over the path for five minutes, while you do so."

"Shouldn't I come with you, ma'am? It's pitch black."

"Do you have a spare lantern?"

Apparently he did, for he lit it for her and by its light, she trudged along the last few yards of road which then narrowed considerably until it was no more than an overgrown footpath. She had come here once when Jane had been very small. She had even carried her down a natural cliff path to a sheltered beach, where Jane had tried to eat the sand while Isabelle had made elaborate castles. It had been gloriously isolated, with no cottages anywhere that she could see.

They had been late home, Isabelle remembered, and she had been scolded by both Elvira and Henry, who had told her the beach was used by cut-throat smugglers and she shouldn't go near it again, let alone take his precious little niece.

"I can't imagine they frequent it during the day," Isabelle had scoffed, immediately sending Henry on to his high horse. Perhaps that was why she had remembered the place. She had already been wrong so often tonight, but this was, surely, the nearest beach to Audley Park for Armand and his men. They would find it easy enough and quiet enough to approach from Finsborough.

The path, the countryside, even the sea, looked different in the dark, quite unfamiliar. When she looked back, she could no longer see the carriage, just a faint glow from its lanterns in the dark. She plodded on, and there, at last, was the shape of cliffs she recalled. It was not far above the beach, not like the cove at the Hart. And there, by their own lantern light, she saw them.

Caron, Boucher, Lefevre, Dupont, and Captain le Noir himself, hauling a boat across the sand by ropes. Four other men watched them.

But despite their concentration and the lights already on the beach, her lantern must have made a difference, for every head turned in her direction.

She had one shot.

Armand released his rope, saying something she couldn't hear. One of the waiting, escaped prisoners ran over to take his place. With peculiar detachment, Isabelle watched him stride across the sand toward the cliff.

She pushed back her cloak and raised the pistol.

"Captain, she's armed!" someone shouted.

He must have heard, but he started climbing.

"I only have one shot," she called in French. "But my aim is true, and your captain is nearest. Leave the boat and follow him up the path. Now. Or I will kill him."

The men at the boat looked at each other and dropped the ropes and began to shuffle hesitantly across the beach.

Armand, however, did not pause until he stood at the top of the cliff facing her. His expression was unusually serious. "You said you would wait for me. Something tells me you haven't decided to come home."

"I have decided to take you back or kill you."

He began to walk toward her once more. There was no fear in his eyes. "Why?"

She stepped back without meaning to. Damn him, *why* was there no fear in his eyes? She *would* shoot him if she had to. "Because you lied to me. You used me. And I don't allow that anymore. Not from anyone. Armand, stand still or I *will* shoot."

His feet didn't even falter. He kept coming. "I didn't lie. *Out of many possible courses, this is the one I chose*…The one that would let me see you again."

Her finger curled around the trigger. "I'm warning you, Armand!"

"I know. But you won't shoot me." He came right up to her until the barrel of the pistol touched his chest. Had she forgotten his utter recklessness? His eyes, as dark and wild as they ever had been, showed no alarm whatsoever. But they glittered with hunger as he bent his head and kissed her.

She gasped into his mouth, and as the pistol dropped between them and slid to the ground, tears wet her face and trickled into their mouths.

"Forgive me," he murmured against her lips. "I didn't see it was selfish or hurtful. I just wanted to see you. Come with me."

She closed her eyes. "I can't."

His mouth claimed hers again. Slowly, his hand slid along her arm to her hand. His other arm was around her waist, and he swayed and turned her as though they were waltzing. Her cloak, her gown billowed around him in the breeze.

"One more dance," he whispered. "Until the next one."

His lips left hers, crept along her cheek, making her shiver with awareness, especially when he reached her sensitive earlobe. "I love you," he breathed.

And then he slipped out of her hold and was running down the path back to the beach. At his yelled orders, his men ran back to the boat.

With a surge of emotion that drowned all thought, all anger, she called after him, *"Bon chance!"*

She could barely see through the tears, but from somewhere, a glow of happiness grew within her. It could only have one cause. *I love you.*

*God help me, I love you, too.* She could not, *would* not be ashamed by that.

One day the war would end. Until then, she could wait.

She bent and picked up the lantern and the fallen pistol. The boat was in the water now, and they were all scrambling inside. Several hands lifted in salute. She raised hers in return, then turned resolutely and made her way back to the carriage.

# Chapter Twelve

Pierre's little house was situated on the edge of fashionable London, behind Russell Square. When Isabelle had stayed there in latter years, it had been when Pierre was absent—apart from one brief, abortive attempt at reconciliation shortly before he died. Usually, she left the Holland covers over most of the furniture, occupying only her own bedchamber and the small sitting room on the ground floor. She saw no reason to change this habit, particularly since she was about to be evicted.

Depressingly, her search for a governess's post was not going well. The agencies she had approached were less than hopeful.

"Nothing in the top rank of society will be available to you," she was told. "You have no references. And then, your name…"

She was almost on the verge of giving in and asking Elvira for a reference, though she shuddered to think what her cousin would write in her hurry to distance herself from the traitor Renarde. Changing her surname back to her father's had at least earned her two interviews with the families of wealthy merchants. One had dismissed her solely on the strength of her looks. The other had insisted she could not live with a foreigner in the house.

On the final morning of October, she sat at her desk in the cramped sitting room, composing a letter of application for a post she wasn't even sure existed. She had heard of it from an acquaintance met by chance yesterday afternoon, who had said her cousin, who lived in

Yorkshire, was hoping to employ a governess for her four children "soon." By this stage, Isabelle felt her best hope was probably to get there first and save the prospective employer from the drudgery of a search. Especially if she dropped in the cousin's name.

When a knock sounded at the front door, she paid it little attention. It was usually tradesmen unable to find their way to the back door to request payment. She left the answering to Mrs. Raisin, her housekeeper, who was more of a maid of all work.

However, a few moments later, the sitting room door opened and Mrs. Raisin, looking impressed, said, "Lord Torbridge asks if you'll receive him, ma'am."

With odd relief, Isabelle replaced her pen in its stand and rose to her feet. "Of course, show him in. And bring some tea, if you please."

Mrs. Raisin effaced herself, and the enigmatic figure of Lord Torbridge strolled in, smiling. "Madame de Renarde," he greeted her, bowing and shaking hands.

"How pleasant to see you, my lord. Won't you sit? Mrs. Raisin is bringing tea."

"Most kind," Torbridge said, taking the chair opposite hers by the fire, which was burning gathered wood rather than expensive coal. "There is a definite chill in the air. How are you after your adventures in Sussex?"

"Refreshed and determined," Isabelle said lightly. "You find me in the midst of an intensive search for a suitable post."

"I hope you have plenty of good ones to choose from?"

Isabelle wrinkled her nose. "I am not overwhelmed with offers. But I have high hopes of this latest application, which is probably ideal, being in the country."

"I hope the salary is satisfactory?"

"I don't know yet," she admitted. "And how are you, my lord? I imagine you are kept busy?"

"Oh, you know me," he said vaguely. He had never actually admitted to doing anything at all in Isabelle's hearing. He just tended to be there in certain situations and take charge. "Actually, while you wait for a suitable offer, I was wondering if you might do me a favor?"

"Of course," she said at once.

His smile was slightly crooked. "I shall not hold you to that until you have heard my problem. Perhaps you are acquainted with Sir Marcus Dain?"

"I don't believe so, although the name is vaguely familiar."

"He is an inveterate traveler. You may have seen his articles in books and magazines. He is also an old friend of mine. In fact, I hope you don't mind that I have asked him to call here so that I might introduce you."

"I am not overwhelmed with callers these days," Isabelle drawled. "I shall be glad to meet your friend. But I am intrigued as to why you asked him, and what he has to do with this favor I agreed to so foolhardily."

"I hoped you would be."

Mrs. Raisin entered with the tea tray.

"Thank you," Isabelle said to her. "We are expecting another gentleman—Sir Marcus Dain. Please just show him straight in."

"Of course, ma'am." Mrs. Raisin looked both impressed and delighted.

"She hopes I will stay," Isabelle said ruefully when the housekeeper had closed the door. "And then she will not be out of work. She doesn't grasp that I can't stay here."

"Even if you earned enough to keep it on?"

Isabelle blinked. "My dear sir, no governess position pays that well! Even if it did, I would get rid of this horrid little house as fast as I could." She lifted the tea pot. "But let us return to Sir Marcus Dain."

"Indeed. He has a brother, a major in Wellington's army on the Peninsula. Sadly, he was injured and sent home to be treated. He and his wife sailed from Lisbon earlier this month. Their ship was attacked by a French frigate, which it saw off, though it took some heavy damage. The captain believed they could limp home and indeed they might have except for the storm... To cut a long story short, they had to take to the longboats. Most made it home, you'll be glad to hear, but Major and Mrs. Dain did not. Thank you," he added, accepting the cup of tea from her.

"Oh dear," Isabelle murmured. "Were they drowned?"

"We thought they must have been, especially when the sailors who had been in the boat with them, turned up rescued by a smuggling vessel. Their boat had broken up against the rocks on the Normandy coast. The men were rescued, but there was no sign of the Dains."

"Go on," Isabelle urged, sipping her tea.

"On Saturday, I received news that they were in fact alive, hiding in a Norman cave near the village of St. Sebastien."

"Well that is great news! I suppose you had that from smugglers, too?"

Torbridge merely smiled vaguely and sipped his tea.

"Did they not bring the Dains home with them?" Isabelle asked.

"No, they couldn't. The problem is, you see, Major Dain is too ill to travel."

Isabelle blinked. "But he is not too ill to live in a cave?"

"He is. Indubitably. But at least the cave has the advantage of shelter and stillness. These smuggling vessels are not large, and at this time of the year, the weather in the Channel tends to be atrocious. She may be wrong, but Mrs. Dain is refusing to move him."

"She'll stay with him till he dies," Isabelle said sadly.

"I'm sure she would. But his brother—you do remember Sir Marcus?—is determined that will not happen. So, I have helped him find a vessel to smuggle him into Normandy."

Isabelle blinked at such casualness. "Will *he* be able bring them both back?"

"By now, if Major Dain is still alive, I imagine the first priority is for him to see a doctor. Bringing a doctor to English people in a cave is an invitation to capture them. We need a longer-term solution. Unless the major is already dead, in which case his wife can simply return with Sir Marcus and the smugglers and the matter will be over."

"And if he is not dead?" she asked, fascinated.

"Then Sir Marcus will have to take a house in St. Sebastian, bring his brother there, and summon a doctor."

Isabelle stared. "I hope he speaks good French."

"He does. He grew up there before the revolution. And I believe their French nurse accompanied them back to England."

Isabell set down her teacup. "Then I wish him all good luck. But where does my favor fit in?"

Torbridge leaned forward. "Well, that is the tricky part. A man on his own is more likely to arouse suspicion. Especially, since I understand Mrs. Dain has very little French. In short, Sir Marcus needs a wife."

Isabelle's mouth dropped open. She barely heard the sharp rap on the front door. "Mrs. Raisin is in need of a new post. *I* am holding out for a governess position. It is still preferable to that of wife."

Torbridge grinned as the sitting room door opened. "It would only be pretend, madame."

"Sir Marcus Dain," Mrs. Raisin announced jovially, and a tall, stern man marched into the room.

Isabelle, gathering her wits and rose to greet him. Lord Torbridge pronounced the introductions, and Sir Marcus bowed with slightly impatient grace. He wanted to get on with the matter in hand.

"Tea, sir?" Isabelle offered.

"Thank you, no. Has Torbridge explained what is required of you?"

Isabelle laughed. It wasn't meant to be a pleasant sound, and it certainly appeared to take Dain aback.

"I have asked Madame de Renarde for her help," Torbridge corrected smoothly. "But she has had no time to consider what this involves."

Rather to her surprise, Dain's harsh face relaxed into a rueful smile. "Forgive me, I am impatient to get on with this. I assumed you were some kind of...employee, under Torbridge's orders."

"I believe I may count his lordship as my friend."

"Then we have that in common. Madam, I am desperate. Do I have your help?"

"I won't deny it's dangerous," Torbridge said. "But I will have a boat waiting for you at all times. St. Sebastien is remote, unimportant, and its inhabitants keep themselves to themselves. I believe this is eminently possible. On top of which, I vouch for Sir Marcus as a gentleman, who has too much honor and too much on his mind besides to make you...uncomfortable."

Isabelle was very conscious of the beating of her heart. France. She would be in France, the country of her birth which had executed most of her family and caused the rest to flee. Without even seeing him, it would somehow bring her closer to Armand.

And on top of everything, the adventure called to her.

"You will be acting for the government of Great Britain," Torbridge added. "And as such, you will be compensated. It *will* be enough to keep this house on."

"I hate the wretched house."

"Oh, I don't know," Dain said, surprising her again by looking about him appreciatively. "It is small, but the proportions are good. I cannot imagine it is decorated to your taste, but a little work would make it much more agreeable."

Isabelle closed her mouth. The man might even be right.

"Your part in the Sussex matter impressed," Torbridge added. "After this business, it is possible there might be more. Unless governessing is your preferred course. But that is for the future. Will you consider helping Sir Marcus?"

Her breath caught. "How long do I have for all this consideration?"

"Half an hour," Torbridge said apologetically. "You will need to catch the next tide."

AND THAT WAS how she came to be crossing the English Channel on a bitterly cold and choppy November night. The first part of the crossing had been spent heaving into a bucket, an indignity of which she was thoroughly ashamed.

However, both the crew and Dain treated her with cheerful sympathy, and when her stomach was empty, suggested she go on deck. And despite the cold and the lashing spray, that was actually better.

She and Dain clung to the rail and discussed their parts as Monsieur and Madame Renard from Paris. They had decided on a name close to her own to make her more comfortable answering to it. And so that the locals wouldn't pry too closely, Torbridge had suggested Dain pretend to be an important employee of the government who had left Paris under a cloud and was now keeping out if the way in St. Sebastien until it all blew over and he was recalled.

"*I don't want to talk about it* works quite well," Torbridge had said. "Or even *I can't talk about it.*"

"I never realized you were so devious," Dain remarked.

"Yes, you did. It's why you came to me. Imply it was a very senior position to account for your superior manners and aristocratic accents. But with luck, no one will wish to talk to you in case your disgrace is catching."

"The dashed physician had better talk to me! Do we know if there *is* one in St. Sebastien?"

"Young and eager, according to my sources," Torbridge said. "But I won't tell you his name. It will look more natural when you ask the townsfolk."

"Someone should have begun the search for our house," Dain said to Isabelle now. "We are to inquire at the solicitor's office in the town square. I suppose we will need to have servants, too, though I'm not keen on having strangers around us all the time."

"If the house is small enough, we can exist very well with one, all-purpose servant. It will keep her too busy to pry."

Dain blinked, but was clearly too gentlemanly to ask if that had been her purpose in London, too. It hadn't. There, she had simply been short of money. He turned, gazing out to sea. "It may not arise," he said abruptly. Meaning his brother might already be dead.

"Then we'll bring your sister home. But I am looking forward to a longer adventure."

Now that her sea-sickness had faded, she found it was true. There had barely been any time to think about what she was doing. But she felt alive in a way she had not since leaving Sussex. Since Armand had sailed away.

Despite her inner happiness caused by his parting words, *I love you*, she'd recognized the danger of simply waiting. Of slipping into a torpor where the past and the future were more important than the present. Searching for a post kept her busy. She had hoped that once she took one up, it would involve her deeply, but she hadn't truly believed it.

This adventure, however, was far more. This was…real distraction.

*Damn you, Armand. Everything comes back to you.* Even though she barely knew him.

THEY LANDED IN the dark, in freezing drizzle. However unpleasant for Isabelle, she could not help fearing for the wounded man and his wife who must have been living in such conditions for most of a week at least.

Several shadowy figures waited on the shore to help pull the boat as far as possible out of the water. Dain chivalrously carried her from the boat to dry land, while all around them was intense activity, unloading the cargo from the boat, and, presumably, reloading it with the crates and barrels already waiting on the beach.

For a moment, she stood still on the sand. *I am in France.* A little thrill surged up from inside her shoes to her spine. After twenty-five years, she stood again on French soil, in the land of her birth.

She hadn't expected it to mean anything. After all, she was here on behalf of her adopted country. But something stirred within her. She just wasn't sure what it was.

Simple fear, probably.

A man detached himself from the flurry. "Monsieur Renard. Madame. Come with me."

There was no farewell exchanged with the crew who had brought them. She and Dain were just another commodity for which, presumably, the smugglers had been paid. Their anonymous new guide led them over a sandy path, then paused to light a lantern, for which Isabelle was unspeakably grateful.

The man, an unshaven, rough individual, perhaps in his forties, raised the light to show them a distinctive hollow in the rock beside them. A pebble lay inside it. The man swiped it off, and it clattered amongst its fellows on the ground.

"When you are ready to depart, leave a pebble in the hollow, and I will know. Come."

The path flattened out, leading them around the coast.

"Aren't you afraid of your light being seen?" Dain asked with a doubtful glance inland.

Their guide shrugged. "Not tonight. The landings are varied between two beaches on either side of the town. Tonight, the soldiers watch the other." His teeth gleamed briefly. "And we watch the soldiers."

"He never mentioned the proximity of soldiers," Isabelle murmured.

"There is a lot he doesn't mention if it suits his purpose," Dain replied. Which was another, interesting way of regarding the amiable Torbridge.

Before long, their guide left the path, which led, perhaps, to a village or to St. Sebastian itself, and walked downward once more. The sea washed over rocks beneath them, battering at the low cliffs of the headland beyond.

Their guide halted, glancing back to make sure they had caught up with him. Then he faced the rock through a mist Isabelle had not noticed before. "Madame."

He wasn't addressing Isabelle. There was a rustle, a movement of frond-like foliage and brush, and a woman peered out.

"Come," she said.

It was doubtful she even saw Dain and Isabelle. Their guide held the foliage aside, and Dain squeezed past Isabelle to step inside before he reached for her hand and helped her inside, too. Their guide entered afterward and replaced the door of hanging foliage and loose branches.

The cave was smoky, but to Isabelle at this moment, it was warm. The reason was an ancient brazier burning in the middle of the chamber, giving off a warm, almost cozy glow. In fact, it was probably smoke from here and not mist she had noticed outside. A pile of rough blankets lay close to the brazier. Someone was helping the stranded couple, most probably their guide.

"Marcus," the woman said hoarsely and all but fell into her brother-in-law's arms. It was a short, desperate embrace for Dain needed to know about his brother.

"Stephen?" he demanded. "Is he...?"

"Ill. Desperately ill." Breaking free, Mrs. Dain dropped to her knees by the pile of blankets and revealed the man within shivering uncontrollably. Isabelle stepped closer and saw a gaunt, unshaven face, eyes closed. By the guide's lantern, sweat glistened on the sick man's face.

"Where is he injured?" Dain demanded.

"There's shrapnel in his side. It's infected, I'm sure, and the reason we were coming home in the first place. And then his leg was broken in the shipwreck. Georges set it," she added, nodding to their guide before she peeled back the blanket to show the splints on either side. "You see why I cannot risk moving him? Even getting him to a boat would be impossible."

"Not impossible," Georges disputed. "Difficult. And painful."

"He doesn't look as if he'd notice," Dain said grimly. Crouching by his brother, he smoothed the damp hair off the burning forehead.

"How did you get him here?" Isabelle blurted.

Mrs. Dain blinked at her, as though noticing her for the first time.

"Madame Renard," Dain murmured, using her slightly altered name. "My sister-in-law, Louisa Dain."

They exchanged curt nods before Mrs. Dain answered the question. "I didn't. *He* got *me* here, even found the cave. I was unconscious." She touched her head as though remembering a pain, or perhaps still feeling it. "I don't like to think of the agony he must have been in, dragging me and that leg..." She shuddered. "And the next day, Georges found us and sent word to England. By then, Stephen was already fevered, and he's only got worse."

"He needs a doctor, Louisa," Dain said heavily.

"Do you think I don't know that?" she burst out. "Even Georges cannot bring a respectable doctor to a cave to treat an English soldier in hiding! There are French soldiers in St. Sebastien."

Dain turned to Georges, asking him in French, "How many soldiers in the town?"

"Not many. They are quartered outside the town, mostly guarding prisoners of war, but they come in now and again. A few new ones have arrived recently to sort out the smuggling problem." He grinned villainously. "But then, why should they? The trade goes both ways."

In both goods and spies, presumably.

"Then they aren't looking very hard?" Isabelle guessed.

Georges shrugged. "An initiative to please the public. The government is seen to be doing something about it. But a British soldier would be carted off to prison, wounded or not, before you could say, *Vive l'empereur*. And *this* prison is no place for officers."

Isabelle regarded him with greater curiosity. "Then why do you help?

Georges smiled. "I am not French." He turned to Dain. "At first light, find the road, about a hundred yards from here directly south. A carriage will wait to take you to St. Sebastien, as though you have just come from Paris. It will leave you there, and from then on, you must take care of matters yourself." He glanced at Mrs. Dain and his eyes softened. This might have been the real reason he helped. "Good luck, madame."

And then he left, carefully rearranging the "door" after himself.

# Chapter Thirteen

Promising to return before nightfall, Isabelle and Dain left the cave at first light and trudged back up to the path. A rather desolate stretch of land greeted them. A few goats chomped on dead leaves and sticks. On the other side of it was a decent road, and just as Georges had promised, a carriage and two horses waited there.

It could not, surely, be waiting for anyone else, and yet Isabelle's feet were reluctant to climb in before confirmation. Dain however, almost hustled her inside and the carriage began to move before he had even closed the door behind them both.

It was not a long journey to St. Sebastian—easily walkable if one did not have to carry a sick and wounded man. The town was just stirring, shutters being thrown open, the odd cart trundling buy delivering milk or eggs to yawning maids and housewives.

The carriage stopped in a pleasant square with a fountain at its center. A large flag hung like a banner over an important building that might have been the town hall, taking up most of one side of the square. On the others were houses and shops, including a baker and a butcher.

This time, the coachman did get down from his box to open the door and let down the steps. Then he retrieved two trunks that had been strapped to the back of the carriage and set them at Dain's feet.

Scowling, Dain was clearly about to deny ownership of the trunks.

"Thank you," Isabelle said hastily. "Pay the man, my dear."

While Dain did so, Isabelle looked about her. The baker's shop threw open its shutters. A woman was washing the windows of a coffee house. Isabelle turned and saw that they had been dropped helpfully at a solicitor's office. *Antoine le Clerque, Notaire*, proclaimed a brass plate beside the door.

"You are right," Dain murmured. "A couple moving from Paris would have more than two carpet bags with them. In fact, we might say we are waiting for the rest of our things to be delivered."

"Do you suppose we have Georges to thank for the trunks?" Isabelle wondered. "Or Torbridge?"

"Let it remain one of the mysteries of life," Dain said sardonically. "And look, here is a useful bench, where we can wait for Monsieur le Clerque's office to open.

Although last night's drizzle had stopped and the sunrise promised a pleasant day, it was still bitterly cold. Dain strolled across to the baker's shop and returned with a warm loaf from which they tore chunks like peasants. It tasted delicious.

Fortunately, the solicitor arrived early, greeted them jovially when accosted by Dain, and had his boy bring the trunks inside his office.

"Of course, of course," he said. "I am delighted to meet you, Monsieur Renard. I had your man's instructions, and I have found you two possible residences—both, sadly, of a temporary nature."

"How temporary?" Dain asked.

"Three months for the first, which you can lease fully staffed." Le Clerque shrugged. "The other for just one month, unstaffed, though there may be the possibility to renew. Also, you may hire the carriage with this house."

"A carriage you say?" Dain pounced. "My wife and I like to go out and about a good deal, so a carriage at our disposal would be ideal. Are there coachmen and grooms?"

"Included in the price of the carriage hire is a coachman, a groom, and a stable lad."

"How large is the house?" Isabelle inquired to dilute Dain's obvious interest in the carriage.

"This one has four bedchambers, two public apartments, and space for three servants in the roof space. Plus the carriage house, of course, where the outdoor servants live. The other house I mentioned has five more spacious bedchambers and three public rooms."

"Let us begin with the smaller," Isabelle said decisively. "For even with the carriage, it is bound to be less expensive."

"It is," le Clerque agreed, standing and reaching for his hat. "We can walk, for it is not far."

THERE WAS NEVER really any doubt that they would take the smaller house, with its carriage all set up, for this would be the quickest, easiest way to bring Major Dain to the house. To make it seem more natural, Isabelle flitted about "the dear little house" gushing her delight with everything.

"Oh, Marc, I have quite fallen in love with this one," she pleaded, clasping Dain's arm. "Please, let us just take it at once! There is no need even to look at the other house. *This* is our new home."

Dain tolerated her raptures very well, exchanging speaking shrugs with the solicitor. "Neither of us can refuse my wife," he said. "This house, if you please, monsieur. With the carriage."

"And would you like me to send staff to be interviewed?" le Clerque asked.

"If you could find us one housekeeper who does not mind getting her hands dirty. And can cook a little," Isabelle said apologetically. "And perhaps a scullery maid?"

Monsieur le Clerque departed with his limited instructions. Dain carried the trunks upstairs, and they opened them to discover a few "personal" belongings. A portrait of a lady from the previous century—"your mother," Isabelle proclaimed, shoving it into his arms—a couple of other pictures of Paris, a few French books including Voltaire and Rousseau and a translation of Payne's *Rights of Man*. There was also extra male and female clothing.

"Thank God," Dain observed. "I left my spare suit of clothes for Stephen." Of course, the officer could not be seen by anyone in his British army uniform.

While Dain stepped around to the attached coach house to make the acquaintance of the staff and horses, Isabelle busied herself with wifely duties, unpacking and putting away their meagre belongings.

An hour later, an urchin delivered a note from the solicitor. The note informed Isabelle that two women would call this afternoon about the housekeeping position. But more importantly, the messenger's arrival gave her the excuse she needed to flit around to the coach house, calling to her "husband" in apparent panic that his brother had been injured climbing the rocks and he must bring him home immediately.

Even Dain looked impressed by that performance. At her clearly over-alarmed demands, he and the bewildered groom constructed a stretcher, and she insisted they all go to retrieve her injured brother-in-law.

As she waved them away, her handkerchief to her mouth, she acknowledged it was going to be wretchedly difficult to maintain this really annoying character if they had to stay in St. Sebastien for very long.

But her heart was in her mouth when she returned inside. She made sure one of the bedchambers was ready to receive him and went down to the kitchen to set water on to boil. They had decided that between them, Dain and Mrs. Dain would carry the major—in his new clothes, his uniform hidden—out of the cave and along to the path. Mrs. Dain had protested vehemently until her brother-in-law had explained the alternative quite brutally. White-faced, she had given in.

From the path, the servants and the stretcher would be summoned, and the major would lie on it inside the carriage to make it easier to bring him indoors.

Isabelle had no idea how long it would take, or even if the major would still be alive when they got to the house. Her concern was genuine when, blessedly sooner than she had dared to hope, the carriage returned and stopped right at the front gate.

She flew out to meet it and was relieved to see the major, muffled in blankets almost to his eyes, being extracted from the carriage on his stretcher. His wife followed, white faced, grubby, and smelling none too sweet. The smoke in the cave must have disguised her fragrance last night, along with her appearance. Now, Isabelle simply flung a cloak around her supposed sister-in-law's shoulders and swept her inside and upstairs to the fourth bedchamber.

"You need a hot bath and a change of clothes," she said briskly.

"I have no time for primping and nonsense!" Mrs. Dain almost exploded. "I have to see to my sick husband."

She almost flounced past Isabelle who caught her arm. "Madam, if you don't play your part, you will have an imprisoned husband or even a dead one, and you will both have endured the last hellish week for nothing."

Mrs. Dain stared at her. If anything, her face grew whiter. But anger still spat from her eyes. Her every instinct, clearly, was to get to her husband. "Who exactly do you think you are?" she demanded intensely.

"I think I am the woman who left her comfortable home to help your brother-in-law save your lives."

Although not *quite* true—that house had never been comfortable—her words had the desired effect. Mrs. Dain blinked. Her eyes fell. One shaking hand came up to touch her forehead, which probably ached. The woman was held together by a very thin thread.

"It's time to let us help," Isabelle said gently. "You have done so much, you can do no more without proper rest. Let Marcus—Marc—make him comfortable for the doctor, while I send up some water for you. And when you're clean and fresh, you can see him before you sleep."

"I will sleep in his chamber!"

"Of course, if you wish it. But not," Isabelle said brutally, "until you are fit to be seen by the doctor, servants, or anyone else not in on the secret. He is supposed to have been injured this morning. Forgive me ma'am, but you look as if you've been living in a cave for a week."

She moved aside, letting Mrs. Dain see herself in the long mirror by the window. A sound that could have been a sob or laughter broke through her lips. "Oh, dear God, so I do. Do I smell, too?"

"Yes," Isabelle said baldly.

"Then I give in. But you will tell me instantly if he takes a turn for the worse?"

"Of course, I will," Isabelle said gently, and went out.

By then, the major had been carried upstairs and transferred to the bed. The three servants were emerging from the bedchamber and clumping downstairs.

"Well met," she said cheerfully. "I need you to carry water upstairs for my sister's bath. Come!"

She directed them to carry up buckets of hot and cold water and leave them outside Mrs. Dain's bedchamber, from where she hauled them inside and helped Mrs. Dain fill the bathtub before the fire. Isabelle gave her some lavender soap and left her to it.

"I'll bring you fresh clothes in just a little," she promised.

With Mrs. Dain taken care of, she knocked on the major's now-closed door and went in. She found his brother had undressed him and was sponging every inch of his skin. She went and took the sponge from him, dipping it in the washbowl and wringing it out.

"Is the doctor sent for?"

Sir Marcus nodded.

"Then you had best shave the major before he gets here. I'll wash him."

Dain made no demur, and they worked together to clean him and dress him more comfortably in a nightgown. By then, he was shivering uncontrollably and tugging futilely at the coverlet. And the doctor arrived.

Dain ran downstairs to let him in.

Isabelle whisked away the bowl of dirty, bloody water and left it in her own chamber while she looked out clothing for Mrs. Dain. She had thought she might have to take up the hem of one of the new gowns, for Mrs. Dain was a few inches shorter. But to her surprise, of the two gowns that had arrived in the mysterious trunk, one was longer than the other.

Impressed, she took the shorter garment, along with some under things and a hairbrush, to Mrs. Dain, who had already climbed out of the bath and was sitting by the fire wrapped in a towel. She looked exhausted, but a lot less deathly pale.

"The doctor has arrived. And here are some things. Do you need help brushing your hair?"

Mrs. Dain shook her head, energized by mention of the doctor, so Isabelle left her to dress, sweeping up the cast-off clothes for washing. Then, her heart in her mouth, she knocked lightly on the major's chamber and went in.

The doctor, a fair, tired-looking young man, looked up from his examination, scowling at the interruption.

"My wife," Dain said hastily.

The doctor nodded curtly and returned to the wound. "How long has it been like this?"

"I'm afraid we don't know," Dain replied. "He hid it from us. Even from his wife. It had healed, as you see, when he returned from Spain."

"Some fragment must have been left inside, either of the shrapnel or of his clothing—it has the same effect. I'll have to cut it open again. If I don't," he added before Dain could even open his mouth to object, "he will certainly die. This is his only chance. Madame, if I might trouble you for hot water and towels."

Isabelle scurried off to obey.

"And his leg?" Dain asked as she left.

"Fortunately, it has been well set and should heal without...."

In the passage, she met Mrs. Dain, looking brisk and determined as she strode to her husband's chamber. Isabelle quickly relayed the doctor's opinion and warned her to let her brother-in-law do the talking for them. The woman only nodded and went in.

IT CAN'T HAVE been easy for either of them, but both Sir Marcus and Mrs. Dain stayed with the major while the doctor worked. Afterward, Dain finally persuaded her to go to her own chamber and rest. When Isabelle looked in after engaging a housekeeper, she was sound asleep.

Dain and Isabelle took turns to sit with the patient, bathe his tight, hot skin, and tip water and the doctor's medicine down his throat. They left him alone only to eat Madame Vosges's first dinner, which was delicious, although Isabelle felt too tired to do it justice. At Dain's bidding, she tumbled into bed and slept until he woke her at about four in the morning.

"I keep falling asleep," he said, clearly angry with himself. "And I'm afraid of missing some change, or the time for his medicine."

"You have to sleep some time. I feel quite rested now and will stay with him."

Obligingly, Dain lit her candle from his own and departed. Since she had no robe with her, she dressed hastily, throwing two shawls about her shoulders and went to the sick man's chamber.

And there, just before nine o'clock, Mrs. Dain found her. The woman was dressed, but only just. Her straw-colored hair hung around her face and shoulders in a mad tangle. "You should have woken me! How is he?"

"You needed the sleep. Marc or I have been with him all night. What do you think? It seems to me he sleeps just a little easier, and his skin is not quite so hot to the touch. Or am I deluding myself?"

"I hope not." Mrs. Dain caressed her husband's forehead and took his hand. He didn't pull it free. His fingers might even have closed around hers, although that could have been an accident. Slowly, she raised her eyes to Isabelle's. "Thank you," she said with difficulty. "I did not say what I ought to have yesterday. Without you and Marcus, I think he would be dead by now."

"Without you, he would assuredly be dead," Isabelle returned. "I don't know how you managed for so long alone." She stood. "If you sit with him, I'll bring you some breakfast."

THE DOCTOR RETURNED in the afternoon and inspected the neatly resewn wound. He gave a grunt of what sounded like satisfaction and applied a clean dressing.

"Carry on," he said in his abrupt way. "I'll return tomorrow."

By then, there really did seem to be some improvement, and they looked at each other in some relief.

Mrs. Dain took her husband's hand and squeezed it. His fingers moved, and he opened eyes that looked almost clear.

"Louisa," he said hoarsely.

Isabelle wanted to weep. Instead, leaving the couple together, she suggested to Dain that they take a walk around the town, both to get some much-needed fresh air and exercise, and to allay the suspicions of the curious.

"I can't believe it is all going so well," she murmured as she took

Dain's arm outside their little house.

"Neither can I," he said in obvious relief. "But by God, I am grateful."

After that, perhaps it was inevitable that it should all go wrong.

As they walked around the square looking in the shop windows as any couple new to the town might do, Isabelle noticed a few soldiers lounging outside the coffee house, presumably enjoying the brief blink of sunshine.

She tensed, making sure not to look at them directly, but it was an effort not to spin around and drag Dain in the opposite direction. Instead, following Dain's lead, she helped make trivial conversation in the quiet, intimate way of couples, their heads close together as they approached the coffee house.

She wasn't sure what made her do it. Sheer nerves, perhaps, or fate. But as they passed the soldiers, she allowed her gaze to flicker just once in their direction. They were officers, and one was staring at her in shock.

Armand le Noir.

# CHAPTER FOURTEEN

WHEN SHE WRENCHED her gaze free, Dain was murmuring. "Be easy. He will just be admiring your beauty."

"He knows me," Isabelle whispered. "He knows who I am." Every instinct she possessed was urging her to turn back to him. Fatal. She allowed Dain to guide her onward, away from him.

"Is he a danger to us?" Dain demanded urgently. "How do you know each other?"

Hastily, stumbling over her words, she blurted out the bare bones of the strange French raid on the Hart Inn to rescue escaped prisoners.

"Then he knows you are a French émigrée. He will, hopefully, just assume that you have come home. Or even that he was mistaken. After all, this is a large country, a large empire. What are the odds of meeting that one man, here in St. Sebastien?"

She stared at him. "Torbridge. Torbridge knew he was here." And he still hadn't given up on his idea of recruiting Armand. And he hadn't even told her, just let them meet to see what would happen. "He manipulated me. Manipulated us all…"

"Oh, nonsense, he cannot be that omniscient," Dain said impatiently. "Or so stupid as to put us deliberately in danger."

Isabelle bit back her retort. She felt as if the whole world was falling in on her, rumbling into fury with Torbridge, fear for Major Dain, his family, and herself, and horrible anxiety over what Armand would think of her. And yet struggling through that maelstrom of emotion came another—excitement because he was here, because she knew she would see him again, somehow. And blind faith that despite seeing her walking so intimately with a tall and personable man, Armand would understand.

ARMAND DID NOT understand.

Not in the slightest. At first, he thought he was hallucinating, his mind playing tricks by placing the face of the woman who occupied so much of his thought, waking and sleeping, onto a complete stranger.

He blinked rapidly, but still Isabelle's lovely face and distinctive golden hair remained. She smiled faintly, causing the familiarly seductive upturn at the corners of her brilliant eyes, which were focused entirely on the tall man at her side. They walked arm-in-arm, their heads close together, comfortable with the intimacy, like lovers or a married couple.

He could not move. And then her gaze flickered to him, as though suddenly aware of the group of men by the café. For an instant, their eyes held in shock, and then the man drew her onward and she looked away, walking on as though nothing had happened.

Nothing had happened? He seemed to explode in a welter of rage and jealousy and sheer curiosity as to what the devil she was doing in France. It had been his dream that she would care enough to come to him when the war was finally over. Unless he could somehow make it safe for her before that, and she could find the courage to risk it.

But to see her here with another man… God help him, that had never entered his head. He had won her for a little on that clifftop. But he was a realist. He'd known he couldn't expect this inconvenient surge of love to last unnourished forever. Yet, he had hoped for longer than a month.

But without doubt, there she walked, already on terms of intimacy with someone else.

Unable to be still, he threw himself out of his seat, threw a coin on the table, and with a muttered word to his companions, strode off in the opposite direction to Isabelle.

Bitterly, he wondered if he could really have been so mistaken in her. Had she been Ashton's mistress after all? If so, he could see no point in her pretense, unless it had been to win him to Torbridge's shadowy cause? And she had tried. But her feelings, her kisses, those had been genuine, he could swear... *Coxcomb, imbecile!* He hurled insults at himself in a fury of hurt and regret, until he stopped dead in the middle of the street without much recollection of how he had got here.

He was missing the important point here. Which wasn't whether or not a woman loved him. But whether she was here to harm his country.

He took a breath, pulling himself together, forcing himself to pay attention. Why had he walked this way instead of following them? Still, the town center was small. He could find them again easily enough. He walked on, until he saw them once more, a tall, distinctive couple with their backs to him.

He followed them at a distance, suppressing another upsurge of jealous rage. They were not talking now, but her hand was still in the strange man's arm. Who was he? Noir did not recall seeing him in the town before, though that meant little. He had not been here long himself, but had been sent to tighten up the smuggling. The government had little objection to British goods sneaking into the country, but they wished to starve Britain of trade with the continent. And they were worried about spies and agents provocateurs entering the country via smugglers' vessels.

Presumably that was how Isabelle had come. Had her companion come with her? Or was he already here? Her victim? Or her ally?

He turned the corner into the Rue de l'Église, just in time to see them walk through a gate and up the path to a pleasant house at the end of the street. The man let himself in with a key, and she followed without looking back.

Pain consumed him, threatening to drown his anger with her. But he wouldn't allow that. He would fall back on duty and find out what he could.

ISABELLE JUMPED WHEN the knock sounded at the front door. She sat alone in the sitting room, for both Dain and Mrs. Dain were with the major. At the ominous sound, she froze, staring at the sitting room door, listening to the hurried tread of Madame Vosges's feet along the passage.

Her heart thundered. *It's him. He's found me.*

While part of her leapt at that wonderful thought, the sane, sensible part was afraid, because he could have brought his soldiers to arrest her. And if she was taken, so would be the fragile major, and everything she and Dain and Mrs. Dain had done would be for nothing. God knew what would happen to them all…

The front door closed, but she could hear Madame Vosges's voice approaching the sitting room door.

*Dear God, she's let him in,* she thought in wild panic. *He has come for me, for all of us.*

The briefest of knocks heralded the housekeeper. "Madame Levigne has called."

Isabelle stared at her, taking a moment to understand that it was not Armand. She didn't know if she was more relieved or disappointed, but by then, a young lady in pink was sweeping past the housekeeper, and Isabelle rose mechanically to greet her.

"Madame, forgive my unexpected call," the lady cried gaily. "I only came to welcome you to St. Sebastien!"

"How very kind of you," Isabelle managed.

"I'm Madame Levigne," the lady explained in such a way that Isabelle knew she was supposed to recognize the name and be gratified. "My husband is the mayor."

"Then I am doubly honored by your visit," Isabelle said hastily. "Won't you sit down? May I offer you refreshment?"

"Oh, no, I shan't disturb you above a moment. I came merely to introduce myself and to ask you and your husband to call whenever you wish." She presented a card of invitation, which Isabelle took with a murmur of gratitude. "I hold quite informal gatherings on Tuesday and Thursday afternoons, so if you can spare the time, I would love to know you better and introduce you to our neighbors."

"Thank you," Isabelle said. Her instinct was to turn the invitation down—surely a sick brother-in-law was excuse enough?—and go nowhere. Never to leave the house until she was dragged away by Armand's soldiers.

But that was not only laughable but foolish. Armand, surely, would do nothing until he had spoken to her. He must owe her that much. And her own and her companions' safety depended on her blending in, on being the people they were pretending to be.

"We should be delighted," she managed, smiling. "It is difficult in a new place where one knows no one."

"Exactly." Madame Levigne laughed. "And now you know me!"

"And I'm very glad to do so!"

"I believe you have come from Paris?"

"Why, yes, we have…"

Madame Levigne stood up. "I shall look forward to hearing all about it, and to meeting your husband, too! Good bye, madame."

"Goodbye—and thank you…"

It was, of course, a good thing. To be accepted by the mayor and his wife would surely raise them above suspicion. If only Armand remained silent. She wrestled with conflicting courses of action, including going alone to the barracks and speaking to Armand. She could tell him the truth, explain about Major Dain. He was bound to be sympathetic. Although his duty must compel him to act against the enemy soldier. Telling him would merely put him in an awkward situation in which duty would win. Nothing he had ever said to her, nothing he had ever done, had led her to believe he would ever ignore his duty.

Her frayed nerves made her start at any outside noise. By the time they had dined, she actively longed for Armand to come, to remove the uncertainty. To be there beside her. Just to talk to him, to see him…

But he didn't come, and she retired wondering desperately what he was doing, what he was thinking.

MRS. DAIN HAD made herself up a bed in her husband's chamber, and in fact, he seemed to be sleeping so much more peacefully that they decided no further watch of the sick man was required. So, Isabelle could have enjoyed a long, undisturbed sleep, if only she had not been tossing and turning instead with anxiety and yearning over Armand.

In the morning, she was delighted to find Major Dain awake and propped up in bed by a sea of pillows. Still deathly pale, he was being fed gruel by his wife and smiled at Isabelle when she entered.

"I remember your face. I thought I was dreaming," he said weakly.

"Madame de Renarde," his wife introduced her. "Whom you must remember to call Isabelle. She is Marcus's wife."

"And he is Marc Renard," the major said with a hint of humor. "I have it now. Except… Are you really his wife?"

Smiling, Isabelle shook her head.

"Pity," the major observed. "I think I've had enough food, Louisa. Where is Marcus? Marc…"

"I'll fetch him for you," Isabelle said. "I'm very glad to see you looking so much better, sir."

DAIN'S RELIEF AT these early signs of his brother's recovery was clearly immense, even though the doctor warned he was not yet out of the woods. He could still die, and there could be no question of moving him anywhere for several more days at least.

And so, they had to fit seamlessly into St. Sebastien. While the major slept later that morning, Isabelle shooed his wife and brother out for a jaunt in the carriage they had insisted on hiring, advising them to walk in the fresh air of the surrounding countryside for an hour. She spent the time discussing food and menus with Madame Vosges and refurbishing her favorite blue, but sadly crushed, day gown for the afternoon.

A knot of nerves seemed to have taken root in her stomach. She needed more to do than primp and set the table for luncheon. But Major Dain only required that she look in on him occasionally while the others were out, and while he slept, she could neither nurse him nor converse with him.

She was delighted by the return of the others, and even persuaded Mrs. Dain to eat luncheon with them before she went to feed her husband.

Dain wrinkled his nose. "Do we have to attend this insipid gathering at the mayor's?" he asked.

"I think we do," Isabelle replied. "It seems to be a sought-after honor. Madame Vosges was certainly impressed! So for us, people supposed to be out of favor with the powerful of Paris, it would look very odd if we did not go."

Dain sighed. "And what if that officer fellow is there?"

"I hope he is," Isabelle said stoutly. "I need to speak to him and find out his intentions."

"At least he hasn't sent his soldiers to arrest us," Dain said. "Presumably, he believes he was mistaken in recognizing you, in which case, why give him more doubts?"

"I thought about that." Isabelle had, in fact, thought about nearly every possibility, endlessly. "But in a town of this size, I'm not sure it's possible to avoid him and still remain above suspicion. He is not a bad man but an honorable officer who is bound to have every sympathy for your brother's plight."

She hoped. In fact, her worst fear was over his suspicion as to why *she* was here.

By the time they walked round to the mayor's large residence, just off the town square, Dain seemed resigned to the afternoon's torture. And the knot in Isabelle's stomach seemed to reach up to her throat. But pretense had become so much part of her character in the years following her disastrous marriage that as soon as the front door opened, she slipped into the role of Madame Renard quite easily.

It didn't stop her heart from jumping into her throat as the servant showed them into the salon. An initial sweeping gaze around the other guests did not reveal Armand, or indeed any officers, which at least gave her a moment to breathe in relief—and to realize that somewhere she was disappointed.

Madame Levigne hurried across to meet them. Today, she wore a soft, powder blue, to match her doll-like eyes. Somehow, she suited all the frills and flounces that Isabelle eschewed, although she was not quite so young as Isabelle had imagined at their first meeting. "Madame Renard, how delightful that you came!"

"My husband," Isabelle murmured. "Marc, our kind hostess, Madame Levigne."

Dain, remembering his French manners, kissed her hand. They were presented with glasses of wine and introduced to several other people, mostly of a class Dain would not normally have encountered socially. Fortunately, he showed no signs of distaste, and Isabelle allowed herself to be separated from him.

In time, she managed to maneuver close to the salon door, for ease of observing other people's departures. In England, a morning call never lasted longer than half an hour, but this appeared to be more of a reception, and she didn't know the customs.

"Madame Renard," murmured a quiet voice behind her.

Her breath caught. Every nerve, every hair on the back of her neck stood up in shock that encompassed both alarm and thrill.

She turned her head and faced Armand le Noir.

Her heart lurched in painful appreciation. In causal civilian dress, he had been a handsome, oddly imposing figure. In the blue, red, and gold military uniform, his magnificence took her breath away. He was not her Armand but some distant, splendid stranger. Panic surged up from her toes, depriving her of breath.

Although he smiled, it did not touch his hard, mocking eyes. "How fortunate you found another husband with a name so closely resembling that of the last one. It must save a lot of confusion."

"You'd be surprised," she managed.

"Armand!" Their hostess fluttered up, throwing out her hand to the new arrival, who kissed it with just a shade too much enjoyment. Madame Levigne fluttered her eyelashes. Her cheeks were prettily flushed. "I was afraid you were going to let me down, but here you have found her already, just as you asked. Madame, allow me to present Captain le Noir, who has been dying to meet you."

"I have," he declared, ushering Isabelle aside and leaving his hostess blinking after them. He handed Isabelle into a chair. But instead of taking the one beside it, he stood looming over her. "For many, many reasons."

She lifted her chin. "And now what? You are going to glower at me until everyone notices?"

"Perhaps. Or at least until your husband notices and calls me out."

"You wish to make me a widow again? Already?"

"You are quite right. Why resort to such drastic action?" He turned, throwing himself into the chair beside hers. "Why are you here, sweet love of mine?"

The sarcasm of his endearment cut her so sharply, she couldn't speak. She gazed straight ahead, a faint, meaningless smile on her lips, as though he bored her. Just as she had sat and smiled at other, much earlier parties when she had found Pierre and his latest mistress also present.

"Why are *you* here?" she retorted into the tense silence between them. "Why did you ask Madame Levigne to invite me?"

"I thought you might prefer it to—er—a raid on your rather charming little house."

"Is that the alternative?"

He held her gaze coolly. "You think me unfair? It's true I asked you to come home. However, I did not invite your husband, and I find I can't ignore him."

She didn't like this new Armand, but just for an instant, she imagined fierce jealousy behind his mocking dark eyes, even in the too off-hand tone of his voice. "You gave me more benefit of the doubt with Maurice Ashton."

"He was a coxcomb. Who is this conveniently named Renard?"

She bit her lips.

"You don't wish to tell me?" he mocked.

"No." *Not here.* It was impossible here. She stood and walked away, her foolish heart in tatters, her mind in such desperate turmoil that she almost bumped into another familiar figure.

"Madame?" said Dr. Ghibert. "Are you well?"

"Oh, yes, of course. How are you, Doctor?"

"Well, as always. I gather your patient is doing better, too? I intend to call in to see him when I leave here in a few minutes."

"My sister will probably be asleep," she said hastily. "But Madame

Vosges will let you in."

"I would not like to wake your sister. Perhaps, if there is no rush, I will leave your patient until the end of the afternoon."

"Perhaps that would be best," she said gratefully, for she trusted neither the major nor Mrs. Dain to convince anyone they were French. This was a difficulty she had not foreseen—and another followed only a few minutes afterward when she glanced toward the door and saw Armand standing there talking with Dr. Ghibert.

The blood drained from her face so fast, she felt dizzy. But this was foolish. The doctor would not discuss his patients with other people. Would he?

Armand glanced across the room at her and smiled.

She wanted to cry, because once she had treasured his smile. It had made her glad and excited, and whatever the situation, she had been unable to resist smiling back. Now, its only purpose seemed to be to hurt her.

*Dear God, when can I leave?*

"Madame Renard, you will ride with us tomorrow, will you not?" The mayor's wife was smiling at her expectantly.

"Ride?" she repeated, trying to pull herself together. "I'm afraid we have no riding horses with us, only the carriage horses we rented with the house."

"Oh, I shall lend you one for the day," said Madame Levigne. "We mean to ride up to the castle ruin on the hill and enjoy the view, which is remarkably fine."

"It sounds delightful. Perhaps I will take you up on your kind offer."

Madame Levigne crowed with delight and linked her arm through Isabelle's to draw her a little apart. "So, what of Captain le Noir, is he not delightful?"

"I'm sure he is perfectly charming."

Madame Levigne was not put off by her coolness. "He was most eager to meet you."

Isabelle glanced at her, distracted by some unexpected note in her voice. The other woman's eyes were limpid blue, quite lovely, and, Isabelle thought suddenly, far too naïve for a woman of her years. Like everyone else, the mayor's wife wore a mask.

Madame Levigne smiled dazzlingly. "You must know I was jealous when he asked me to invite you. Every lady wants Captain le Noir in her court. So dashing, so brave and handsome."

"And whose court is he in?" The words seemed to be wrung from her. She forced a smile. "Yours, I imagine."

Madame Levigne laughed and tapped her wrist with her fan. "Discretion, my dear! Oh, monsieur..." She flitted off again, leaving Isabelle to wonder if she had just been warned off by the same woman who had thrown her in Armand's path.

If they were lovers... Her fist clenched at her side, and she had to force her fingers to unfurl, to ignore the pain. If they were lovers, then Madame Levigne was not secure in her position.

*What a perfect end to this awful party. At least, please let it be the end!*

A quick glance showed her Dain deep in conversation by the fireplace. Continuing her sweep, she came upon Armand, alone now, observing her.

This was unbearable.

In sudden decision, she walked across the room to him. He watched her coming, his face unreadable.

"I need to talk to you," she said abruptly.

"Here I am."

"Not here. Everyone is staring, waiting for us to make an adulterous assignation—at the very least—right under the nose of my husband."

"Ah, yes, your husband of three weeks, or is it four? With whom you somehow managed to thrive in Paris before his unexpected disgrace."

By an effort of will, she prevented her eyes from darting around to see who could have overheard him. "You know who I am," she said painfully. "There is no need to bait me."

"No? Then what do you suggest?" He bowed. "Don't bother. I will find a way as always. Madame." He strolled away toward his hostess without a backward glance.

# CHAPTER FIFTEEN

THE REST OF the day was, for Isabelle, miserable and depressing. The most assurance she could give to Dain was that she didn't believe her acquaintance had yet given them away, and that he *probably* wouldn't, at least until she had explained matters to him.

The question was, what did she tell him?

She had not yet lied to him. Merely, he had picked up the lies that had been fed to other people. Her initial instinct had been to lay the whole matter at his feet and beg his silence. But this man, this stranger, was no longer her reckless, passionate Armand who had whispered *I love you* into her ear on a wind-swept cliff top. And she could not trust him.

After dinner, her companions went to keep the major company in his bedchamber. Isabelle retreated to the sitting room alone, trying to think how best to proceed. If they should risk Major Dain's life and simply go home, which could, in fact, be the lesser of the evils currently confronting them. She veered away from personal concerns, ignoring the almost physical pain clawing at her heart.

She hadn't known him. She hadn't known him at all.

Dr. Ghibert was pleased with his patient's progress. Surely, if she could just buy Armand's silence for two more days, they could just take Major Dain and go home. And if they succeeded, perhaps she would take up Lord Torbridge's offer of future employment—with the stipulation that France itself was excluded from her duties.

Torbridge. What exactly did he expect her to do with Armand le Noir? As things stood between them, she had less than no influence over the captain, and she was quite sure he never had any intention of doing Torbridge's bidding in any case. Insane to have put them all in danger like this, where one word from Armand would have them all clapped up. What in God's name was his obsession with one relatively lowly and extremely loyal enemy officer?

A knock at the door made her jump. She stared at the window. It was long past the hour of social calls without specific invitation. Her heart in her mouth, she strained to hear the sounds of voices, marching feet. Was it a good sign she heard none?

The sitting room door opened. "Ah, you are still up, madame," the housekeeper said. "Do you wish to receive Captain le Noir, or shall I send him away until tomorrow?"

Her stomach twisted. She had known it was him. But at least he had come alone. "I will see him. I'm sure he won't be long."

Radiating disapproval, the housekeeper stood aside for Armand. "Shall I inform monsieur?"

Aware only of Armand sauntering into the room, Isabelle said hastily, "Not specially. I'm sure he will be down momentarily. Thank you, that will be all."

The door closed quietly behind Madame Vosges, leaving her alone with Armand. She rose to her feet, her heart drumming with nerves as he walked across the room and halted only inches from her.

She still could not read his face, but at least, in private, she remembered it. The golden skin from a life spent largely outdoors, faint crows' feet at the corners of his turbulent eyes, the lean, almost hollow cheeks, those expressive, sensual lips that had kissed her so sweetly, so...

"You had better tell me everything," he said abruptly.

"Or what?" she challenged. Unwisely, perhaps, but his command irritated her.

"There is no *or what*, no alternative," he said impatiently. "That man, who is almost certainly not called Renard, is not your husband, and you have not entered France legally. If you want my help, or even my silence, you must tell me why,"

Put like that, it was not unreasonable. She felt her shoulders droop and hastily pulled them back. Wordlessly, he took her hand. It jumped in his, but he only returned her to the sofa, and she sat almost without realizing it.

He sat beside her, turned toward her with his arm resting along the back of the sofa behind her. Hemmed in. In every way. He was right. She had no choice. And no made-up story could be better than the truth.

She drew a deep breath and looked at her clasped hands in her lap. "You are right. Monsieur Renard is not my husband. He is an English gentleman as I'm sure you have already guessed. His brother is a British army officer, wounded and sent home, but then shipwrecked and washed ashore in France."

"He will be the sick man being treated by Ghibert."

He knew everything already, it seemed. She raised her gaze to his. "His wife was with him. His leg was broken and his wound corrupted, causing a severe fever. She was afraid to move him. And so, we travelled here secretly to ensure he became well enough to travel. Or to bury him and bring his wife home."

"A married couple renting a house being so much less suspicious than one man living in a tent on the edge of town," he guessed. "But what is your connection to these men? Family?"

It would have been easier to nod. But she would not lie. "Lord Torbridge," she said reluctantly.

"He knew I was here?" Armand's eyes were steady, unthreatening and yet quite opaque. She had no idea what he was thinking, let alone feeling.

"I think he did."

He took that in with the same impassivity. Then, abruptly, he jumped to his feet and began pacing, and here at last was something of the Armand she remembered. At the window, he swung around to face her. "Will he live? The brother?"

"He is improved," Isabelle said carefully. "Dr. Ghibert seems hopeful but has not yet committed himself."

He strode back toward her, frowning. "How did you get here?"

"Much the same way as you, I imagine."

"And I presume you plan to leave in the same manner. The irony is, I am here to stop the smuggling along this part of the coast. You expect me to give up promotion again?"

Encouraged by his straight-faced humor, she allowed herself to answer back. "I suspect you're more likely to get recognition by leaving the smugglers alone. They are at least as useful to you as they are to us."

"That is sadly true. But one picks one's way through to achieve the desired result. For a week or so, at least."

"Can it wait until we're gone?"

He held her gaze. "When will you go?"

"When our patient can be moved. Or earlier if it becomes necessary."

"You expect me not to make it necessary?"

"We let you and your men go. Even with your escaped prisoners in the end."

"You followed me with a pistol to prevent me," he pointed out.

"If it makes you feel better, you can follow us with one, too, though I'd rather you didn't use it."

For the first time in France, she heard his breath of muted laughter. Their eyes met and held, and a glimmer of hope flickered through her veins. Perhaps he was merely angry, feeling betrayed and manipulated, as she had been the night of the Audley Park ball when he had finally left England. Perhaps.

She caught her breath. "Armand—"

"I have to go." He swung away from her toward the door, and she sprang up after him. "I have smugglers to chase, and I don't want to upset your marriage."

"Armand, don't!" Impatiently, she seized his arm and he spun around to face her. Too close. Much too close. She could feel the warmth of his body, smell his familiar, clean, earthy scent, make out every detail of his skin, of his suddenly desperate, clouded eyes. She couldn't breathe.

Her hand dropped to her side, and she stepped back, but it made no difference. He followed her, standing just as close yet still not touching. His turbulent eyes, no longer masked, lowered to her lips, and butterflies soared in response. She could feel his quickened breath on her cheek, her lips as if he had bent toward her, or she had tipped her face closer to his.

And then he flung away from her. The door opened and closed so fast it left a draught. She heard the front door all but slam behind him, too, and then his tall, lean figure, strode past the window.

He was gone, with nothing right between them.

But nothing felt quite as wrong as before.

UNWILLING TO GO into details about her conversation with Armand last night, Isabelle told Dain only that she thought they were safe for now. They were breakfasting at the time, and Isabelle was dressed for riding in order to join Madame Levigne's party.

"Will *he* be there?" Dain asked, frowning.

Her heart leapt at the thought, even though she had wondered about it too often already. "I don't know," she replied calmly. "It's possible, I suppose, but he does have military duties."

Dain nodded curtly. "Well, keep him sweet, if you can, without…endangering yourself."

"Of course," she muttered and fled, unsure whether the emotion bursting out of her was laughter or sheer, sudden lust. It had been so long since she'd known a man's embrace…And neither of those men had been Armand le Noir. If he made love as he kissed…

Hastily, she diverted her thoughts. Her purpose today was not to flirt with Armand, let alone seduce him—if he was even present! It was to play her part of belonging to this town, this country, so that Major Dain could recover enough to return home. So, although she could not like Madame Levigne, not her girlish frills or her mask of fun-loving innocence, nor whatever calculation lay beneath, she walked around to her house and smiled as though there was nowhere else she would rather be.

The party consisted of Madame Levigne, who invited Isabelle to call her Lucie, Lucie's swaggering young brother Auguste, two of the younger women who had been present yesterday afternoon, and two army officers, neither of whom were Captain le Noir. They were Lieutenants Linville and Bernard.

Noir's absence was not lost on Lucie, who pouted at the officers and demanded to know, "Where is my Armand?"

Which grated on Isabelle's ears. Was it his own faithlessness that had made him suspect hers?

"He's sleeping," Lieutenant Bernard replied. "He was on duty all night. But he says he may catch us up later."

"I hope you told him Madame Renard is with us," Lucie said archly. It felt like a barb. As though he were pointing out Isabelle's presence was not enough to make him stir out of bed. In which case, of course, neither was Lucie's.

They rode out of St. Sebastian to the east, in the opposite direction to the one Isabelle knew and then turned inland across country. It was a pleasant day to be outdoors—bright, sharp, and cold—and Isabelle was happy to be able to give her spirited mare her head.

It was pretty countryside, with rolling farmland and gentle hills, interspersed with thick woods and burbling streams. What was left of the ruined castle they had come to visit stood on a rise slightly higher than the others, enough to provide a spectacular view in all directions. Everyone dismounted to admire it, leaving the horses free to rest and crop the grass and other foliage in the vicinity.

In wonder, Isabelle turned a full circle, drinking it all in—St. Sebastien laid out before the sea, farmhouses and little churches dotted among the well-kept land, fields of cows, sheep and goats, long, winding streaks of roads, and glistening streams, a majestic river joining up several of the villages in the distance.

*France.*

Her throat closed up as it had threatened to do when she had first landed. It wasn't home. But she felt *something*, some recognition, some awareness. The king, the national convention, Bonaparte, whoever or whatever followed—all had come and would go, like war and peace and revolution, famine and prosperity. And through it all, France remained.

And maybe, just maybe, she could forgive Pierre his betrayal of England for France. Not that she would follow in his footsteps. For one thing, she was sure he had done it mostly for personal, monetary gain. Still, to some degree at least, it had been for this country, this land, these people.

"Captain Armand!" Madame Levigne's playful greeting gushed over her, snapping her attention back to her more immediate surroundings.

Armand arrived among them, reining in from a gallop up the hill, to be greeted by a flurry of jokes from the other officers and the excited adulation of the ladies who, of course, took their lead from the mayor's wife. With him, a surge of energy seemed to sweep through the little gathering, even to Isabelle who stood a little apart to enjoy her first sight of the favored scenery. It was more than his handsome person, although that helped. Even at the Hart, trying to blend in at first, he had possessed a magnetism that had, perhaps, been the cause of the attention and suspicion that had led to his disastrous duel with Lieutenant Steele. Here, with permission to flourish, it hit Isabelle like a blow.

He greeted the ladies, smiling and responded to the jokes of the men, made some general remark about the view, and then strolled around, somehow shedding the women almost hanging on his arm before he walked inexorably toward Isabelle.

Aware of his approach, she kept her gaze on the view. Last night's almost understanding, almost embrace, clung to her mind, trying to dislodge her appreciation of the scenery. She had no idea how he would be with her, what he would say, what he thought.

He did not bow or even greet her. So, she didn't acknowledge him either as he stood beside her, apparently also admiring the view.

"So, what do you think of France?"

"I think this small part of it is very beautiful."

"Where did your people come from?" he asked with what sounded like genuine curiosity.

"South. The Dordogne. Mostly."

"Will you travel to see it?"

She blinked, turning to him in surprise. "Of course not. I have no time. Nor inclination. I neither know nor care who holds my old home now."

"Then you feel nothing for the land of your birth?"

She dragged her gaze free of his. "Not nothing. But it is not my home."

"Neither, I think, is England."

A faint smile tugged at her lips. "The curse of the exile."

"It is not impossible for you to stay. My foster father, who I told you about, has influence enough to smooth everything over."

She felt his gaze burning into her face. "And then the country that nurtured me when my own would have killed me, becomes my enemy."

"We need peace," he said flatly.

"Is it any more likely?"

"Perhaps. The emperor is retreating from Moscow. Such failure does him no good, and it will get worse as the winter closes in. It will take months to get the army home, and God knows what state it will be in."

He had comrades, friends in that massive army. She thought he was already grieving for them. Then, just when he had won her sympathy, he said abruptly, "I want to see him."

"The emperor?" she said blankly.

His lip twitched. "Your wounded soldier. If you want my silence, I must see who and what he is."

She stared at him. "You are not a trusting man, are you, Captain le Noir?"

"I don't believe you are a trusting woman, Madam Renard." With exaggerated politeness, he offered his arm, and she took it to avoid the appearance of rudeness. All the same, there was a secret thrill in touching him, emphasizing her gnawing need to know where they stood. If his last words to her in England were true.

No, she wasn't a trusting woman.

Since they were going to ride on to an inn where Madame Levigne had ordered luncheon, Armand boosted Isabelle into the saddle first. Just as she had done earlier, the spirited mare tossed her head, performing a brisk, swaying little sidestep with the aim of dislodging her rider before she was secure in the saddle.

Isabelle held firm, tightening the reins until the mare snorted and submitted. With the leisure now to glance at her fellow riders, she found Lucie Levigne's oddly assessing gaze upon her. There was a discontented curl to those pretty lips, though it vanished at once into a sizzling smile.

"What a fine rider you are, Isabelle. Did you have so much practice in Paris?"

"In Paris, not really. I was brought up in the country. How far is the inn from here?"

The subject was effectively changed, but Isabelle harbored the suspicion that Lucie, who rode a well-mannered, docile animal, had chosen the livelier, more spiteful mare for Isabelle in order to show the newcomer to disadvantage.

Isabelle wondered if she should allow herself to fall off to please the mayor's wife.

She spent almost the whole journey to the inn hemmed in by Lucie's brother, Auguste, and one of the officers, Captain Linville, who vied with each other for her attentions. For the first ten minutes, it was amusing, and she jested with them both. After half an hour, she felt so constricted, she wanted to scream.

It didn't help that she could see Armand in front riding beside Lucie. She had to keep reminding herself that she was here to be friendly to all and prevent any suspicions arising about her "family." Not to give set-downs and act as though she were immeasurably above her foolish companions. Nevertheless, she approached the inn with considerable relief and attached herself to the other women as closely as she could during the time they spent there.

"Where next, divine Madame Lucie?" Lieutenant Bernard demanded jovially as he sat back in his chair.

"You are planning to go further?" Isabelle asked, dismayed.

"Absolutely," Lucie enthused. "There is the most beautiful medieval church in—"

"I must leave that treat for another time, sadly," Isabelle interrupted, "I must return to St. Sebastien this afternoon."

"Why?" Lucie asked blankly.

"My brother-in-law is in his sick bed and needs nursing. I have promised to return in time to give his wife some rest."

"Oh, I'm sure she won't mind for once," Lucie said carelessly. "Come with us, for you can't go home alone."

"Of course I can. I have an excellent sense of direction."

"But you *will* not," Armand declared. "I shall escort you."

"There is no need," Isabelle said hastily, only too aware of the daggers spitting at her from Lucie's eyes.

"There is every need, and I am no loss to your party, Madame, since I, too, have to return." He lowered his voice, murmuring something in Lucie's ear.

A faint smile dawned on her discontented face. A few more teasing words, and she laughed, playfully slapping Armand's wrist. "You are a wicked man! Very well, you may go, too. Goodbye, Isabelle! You must come to Monsieur le Maire's birthday reception—I shall send you a card."

With massive relief, Isabelle mounted the mare in the inn yard once more. "Do you really need to go back this afternoon?" she asked Armand.

He shrugged, urging his horse toward the inn gate. "I want to. Frankly, an hour of such company is enough."

"And yet you flirt well enough with it," Isabelle retorted.

"I had the impression you wished to avoid ill-feeling."

"What on earth did you say to her? If it won't make me blush."

"I only promised to return your mare to her."

She glanced at him skeptically, and he laughed. "Come, we shall go the direct route."

Although shorter and less picturesque, the journey back to St. Sebastien was much more comfortable. They talked only of impersonal things, and yet there was wit and fun in the way he expressed himself, the deep passion of his character occasionally breaking out with a surge of enthusiasm or disgust. Isabelle could not help but respond, and the road flew by in enjoyment of his company, until before she expected it, they were back in St. Sebastien.

The reality of her situation began to close around her once more, slowing her tongue and her laughter. But she had had time to think, and as they turned into the Rue l'Église, she said abruptly, "Come tomorrow morning to meet the major. It will give his wife—"

"I will meet him now," Armand interrupted.

She frowned at his implacable voice. "But that gives us no time to—"

"Exactly."

There was a hardness behind his eyes that made her shrivel, even as she lifted her chin in defiance. He knew from Dr. Ghibert that the patient existed, but he wanted an honest reaction to his presence, an unprepared meeting from which to make his judgement.

"You are most certainly not a trusting man," she said coldly.

# Chapter Sixteen

W HEN SHE OPENED the front door with her key, Sir Marcus Dain was just coming out of the sitting room, a folded newspaper in his hand.

"Ah, how was it?" he asked in careless English.

Armand stepped in behind her and smiled. "Monsieur."

Dain's gaze flew to hers. Armand shut the door deliberately.

"He knows," Isabelle said flatly. "He has told no one, but he wants to speak to you and your brother. And, no doubt, Louisa."

Dain drew himself up to his full height, which was more or less level with Armand's, his expression one of aristocratic disdain. And then he opened his mouth.

"Don't even trouble to defy me," Armand said curtly. "The alternative for all of you is unthinkable. But by all means, lead the way."

Dain's eyes narrowed. "So, you are the fellow who kept an inn full of women and children at gunpoint all night?"

"It wasn't full, and I had help. Lead on, monsieur."

"Marcus," Isabelle said quietly.

Without a word, Dain turned on his heel and marched upstairs. Armand followed him, and after an instant's hesitation, Isabelle went after them. She was the only one who knew all concerned.

With a brief knock, Dain opened his brother's bedchamber door a crack, then turned as if to block the Frenchman's entrance. Before anyone could guess his intention, Armand simply reached beyond him, shoved the door wide, and walked in.

"Good evening," he said in cheerful English. "Madam, please excuse the unannounced visit. How are you, Major...?" He trailed off on a question, clearly asking the major's name.

The invalid and his wife, looking understandably confused by the entrance of an obviously French officer, glanced wildly at Dain and Isabelle who had all but fallen into the room behind Armand.

The major, pale and sickly beneath the tan of his skin, said hopefully, "Renard?"

As a performance of his new character, it was poor, and it made Armand grin.

Isabelle stepped forward. "Perhaps it would be simplest if I made the introductions? Allow me to present Captain Armand le Noir, who is...an acquaintance who owes me a debt."

"Do I indeed?" Armand drawled.

Isabelle ignored him. "Sir, Major and Mrs. Dain. And Sir Marcus Dain."

Armand bowed. Sir Marcus and Mrs. Dain glowered, the latter with more than a hint of alarm.

The Frenchman, ignoring the hostility, perched on the end of the major's bed. "Where were you wounded?" he asked sympathetically. "Badajos?"

"No, got through that without a scratch, though God knows how. This was from a mere skirmish, took both sides by surprise, but I took a scattering of shrapnel."

"Bad luck. It can take ages to get all of it out."

"I think the surgeon missed some. They sent me home for some proper excavation, but, well, we haven't quite made it."

While they talked, Sir Marcus and Louisa looked rather helplessly at Isabelle for further explanation. But she had none except what they all saw and heard. Two officers, enemies, chatting about wounds and battles in Spain. They discovered they had fought each other at

Fuengirola in 1810, even discussing ways in which the day could have gone against the French. Armand told an amusing tale of his narrow escape from capture that day, and the major laughed.

By then, however, he was looking exhausted, and Armand stood up, taking in, Isabelle noticed, Louisa's clear anxiety for her husband.

"I wish you a speedy recovery," Armand said. "Though I don't want to meet you in battle now. Mrs. Dain." He bowed and casually left the room.

Isabelle bolted after him. At the foot of the stairs, he made straight for the front door until Isabelle almost exploded after him.

"Armand! You cannot leave us like this!"

He swung to face her, scowling. His eyes looked angry as they clashed with hers. Then he threw up one hand and all but stalked into the sitting room.

"Well?" Isabelle demanded, closing the door behind them and leaning on it. "Will you let us stay until he is well? Will you let us go?"

Armand strode up and down the room like a caged beast. "He would die in prison," he snapped. "And the rest of you have no business here. And for that, I am to betray…"

"No more than you asked Lieutenant Steele to betray when he let you go."

"He kept the damned prisoners."

"And you came back for them. You couldn't have done that if he'd called the soldiers after you."

Furiously, he waved that aside and kept prowling, from side to side and back.

"Armand," she said gently. "I think your decision was made that first day when you didn't send soldiers after me."

He paused, staring at her. "You are different."

"Because I'm a woman?" she challenged.

"Because you're mine," he ground out. He took the distance between them in two strides and seized her in his arms, hard against his body, making her gasp. And then his mouth crushed hers in a kiss so overwhelming, she would have collapsed if he hadn't been holding her so tightly.

Her surrender was total, immediate, and blissful. He devoured her mouth with lips and tongue and teeth, as if he would never stop, and yet when she struggled feebly in his hold, he began to release her. With a sob, she threw her arms up and around his neck and kissed him back. A growl of triumph rose up his throat, vibrating his chest against her breasts.

Lost in him, she did not even hear the door opening.

"What on earth!" Sir Marcus exclaimed, striding across the room. "Sir, you will answer to—"

Still stunned, Isabelle found her lips free at last. She grabbed for her wits and stepped back from Armand's only loosened embrace.

"Oh, stop it, Marcus!" she said irritably. "You forget you are not really my husband."

Dain stopped in his tracks, frowning. "No, but I still stand as your protector. And this libertine taking advantage of—"

"There is no question of such things," Isabelle said hastily, for Armand seemed more inclined to laugh.

"I am almost sorry," Dain snapped. "For if I shot him in a duel, it would kill two birds with one stone!"

"There will be no duels," Isabelle pronounced. "No one has been injured. And Captain le Noir is leaving."

"You just asked me to stay," he protested from sheer devilment.

Isabelle narrowed her eyes. "To discuss Major Dain."

"Major Renard," Armand corrected.

"Is he enjoying this?" Dain demanded.

"Immensely," Isabelle replied, taking the captain's arm and urging him past Dain to the open door. He allowed himself to be removed, even going so far as to wish Dain a polite goodnight.

But in the hall, as she reached for the front door, the rollicking look faded from his eyes, leaving them thrillingly warm and serious. He cupped her cheek in a tender caress. "We will find a way," he said softly.

She held his rough hand against her skin, inhaling its scent of horse and leather and sheer Armand. "I know."

And then he was gone, letting himself out and closing the door behind him.

She walked rather slowly back to the sitting room, for she did not wish to discuss this now.

"How is your brother?" she asked.

"Asleep. Louisa is with him. He likes le Noir. I'm not sure I do."

"There is much that is likeable. And I suspect there is understanding between all soldiers that excludes us lesser mortals."

"Perhaps." He seemed to hesitate, then said gruffly, "You do not need to take this so far. I wish you would not. Neither my brother nor Louisa would wish it either."

Isabelle went and sat by the fire, gazing into the flames for a few moments before she glanced back to him. "My relationship with Captain le Noir has nothing to do with our situation here or with your family. It is an impossible relationship, and yet it exists."

Dain was silent until he, too, sat down, choosing the chair on the opposite side of the fire. To anyone looking in, they would appear to be a comfortably married couple.

"You are in love with him," Dain said quietly.

Isabelle returned her gaze to the flames and nodded. It tied her heart and stomach in knots, but there was no other way to describe the beautiful, terrible ache within her. She drew in her breath. "It does not affect our plan."

"Does it mean we have a friend?"

"Yes," she allowed. "But one of whom I will not take more advantage."

SHE LOVED HIM.

He woke with the elation of this knowledge, even as the smell of coffee filled his nostrils and he became aware of Caron's presence in the room. A candle still burned on the table, for it was not yet quite light.

Noir stretched and yawned prodigiously. "Morning, Caron! What news?"

"Morning, Captain. Got a smuggler last night. And you've got two letters."

"Good news all round!" Noir threw off the blankets. "I'll be down to see the prisoner directly."

Dunking his whole head in the washing water, which Caron hadn't troubled to warm, could not damp his high spirits, though it did help to remind him that love was not enough for them to be together. She was still in danger, and he was suppressing knowledge of an enemy presence. At this moment, he did not care. He was happy and would live for the day.

While watching out for her.

He dried his washed body thoroughly and sang to himself as he shaved. He grinned at the crash of a boot hitting the other side of the wall, but only sang louder. Which led to a slight nick under his chin, but at least it didn't bleed much.

Throwing himself into the chair by the table, he reached for the coffee pot and eyed his two letters. One was perfumed and tied with pink ribbon, directed in an almost childish hand. The other, emblazoned in bold, familiar letters was from the man who had given him a name, an education, and a value to himself and the world. Communications from him were not always undiluted pleasure, but they were generally interesting. In this case, he doubted even that, for he had ignored the last two summonses and the abbé would be miffed.

With a sigh, he reached for the perfumed missive which was, as he'd suspected, from the mayor's wife, thanking him prettily for returning her dear Isabelle's borrowed horse to the stables, but expressing disappointment he had not called on her afterward. Perhaps he could rectify this serious omission during the morning? And by the way, she hoped he had remembered the mayor's birthday reception, which would not be complete without his presence.

Noir dropped the letter in vague irritation. If the silly girl had to look beyond the mayor, he wished she'd fix her interest on some other man. He had never had any intention of playing that game with her. For one thing, she was far too vapid. For another, Isabelle de Renarde had filled his heart since he'd returned from England, and it seemed she had spoiled him for other women.

He broke the seal on the other letter and unfolded it. Disappointingly short, it was, as he'd suspected, little more than a summons, urgent in tone, together with the assurance that his leave was approved by his superiors. And as usual, it was signed only T. Which was why Noir normally addressed him simply with his initial, too. When he wished to be formal, he called him Abbé T.

Noir scowled at the missive. But in truth, nothing could spoil his happiness right now, and even as he finished his coffee, he knew he had no intention of going. Not until matters here were resolved. Not until she was safe.

Crumpling a letter in either hand, he threw Lucie Levigne's in the fire and stuffed his foster parent's in his coat pocket before leaving his quarters. He had already begun to sing again. On impulse, he walked in the wrong direction, threw open his neighbor's door, and blasted him with a few climactic notes, only just managing to close it before the boot struck it with painful force.

Laughing, he went on his way. He was still humming below his breath as he entered the prison area of the fortress.

Boucher was there, playing dice with one of the other men. On sight of him, they both leapt to attention.

"Good morning," Noir greeted them cheerfully. "Who do we have then?"

Boucher trotted off to the cell along the passage.

"He won't talk to us," the other soldier said. "Maintains he doesn't smuggle, never sails beyond the shallows and was only fishing when we picked him up."

"Does he have a name?" Noir asked, sitting and sweeping the dice into the drawer beneath the table top.

"Georges. But whether it is surname or no—or even his name—is anyone's guess."

Boucher dragged the bedraggled prisoner into the room, and the man glanced warily around his captors.

Noir cursed and stood up. "He's one of ours! Let him go."

"Thought he looked familiar," Boucher remarked. He should have been. He had been part of the crew that brought them home from England last month. "Thing is, though, we know a shipment of brandy went out last night, and he'd no other call to be on the water."

"You'd have been better stopping the brandy than Monsieur Georges here."

"We were too late. Most of us were at the other side of St. Sebastien."

Noir glared at his prisoner. "Why do you have to be so annoying? Can't you just help your country?"

"Got to make a living somehow, Colonel."

"There's no point in flattering me with promotion. I like being a lowly captain." He tapped his finger against his lips, looking from the prisoner to his own men. "Damn it, we can't keep him," he said at last. "If we break up their network, some poor French devil will be left stranded on some English beach."

"You think he's that important?" Boucher asked doubtfully.

"I don't know," Noir admitted. "But he does keep cropping up.

Come on, Georges, I shall give myself the pleasure of kicking you out."

Georges grinned, jumping up with alacrity. Noir bowed him out of the room ahead of himself.

As they walked up the stone steps and along the passage, Noir said, "Tell me, Georges, do you ever smuggle British people into France?"

"Oh, no, sir," George exclaimed, apparently shocked. "Like you say, sir, I'm one of yours."

Noir turned and met his gaze. "Then you wouldn't know anything about a wounded British officer? Or his family."

Georges held his gaze steadily. "Never smuggled any such into the country. Ever."

It might have been the truth. But the careful wording was suspect.

No one had smuggled Major Dain or his wife into France. Nature had done that. Perhaps Georges hadn't brought Isabelle and her supposed "husband" either, but Noir suspected he had something to do with it. Which was another reason to let him go. Sooner or later, they would need him again.

An uncomfortable twinge of guilt pierced his happiness. But it was easy enough to squash, for nothing in the world would convince him to endanger Isabelle.

NOIR SPENT THE next two hours writing a report of the task to date, stating frankly that, while they had cleaned things up to some degree, the smuggling in the area was so entangled with covert operations and intelligence gathering that he recommended shelving further investigation until peace time. He suggested they would accomplish everything possible or sensible within the next two weeks.

By which time, he devoutly hoped, Isabelle would be well clear of danger.

Thinking of whom…

Seizing a fresh piece of paper, he dashed off a note, sealed it, and directed it to Madam Renard in the Rue l'Église. Then, grabbing his coat, he left the office. "I'll be back in the afternoon," he called to the duty guard. "Captain Kronberg is in charge."

On the way to his quarters to change, he sent Dupont off with his note to Isabelle. But as he turned, he found Lieutenant Bernard watching him with suspicion.

"Well?" he demanded.

"Are you writing to her?" Bernard demanded.

Armand stared at him. "It's none of your damned business who I write to."

Bernard flushed. "Of course not. Merely… Captain, where do you stand with the divine Lucie? I would not tread on your toes, but I am serious in my—"

"Don't be," Armand interrupted. "For she isn't. If she ever leaves the mayor, it will not be for the likes of either of us."

Bernard started angrily, "Then you merely trifle with the lady?"

"Oh, take a powder," Armand exclaimed. "I've never even tried to lay a finger on her and never will."

Bernard's face relaxed into smiles. "Then you will not mind if I…"

"I advise you not to, but the rest is up to you," Armand said and walked away.

Half an hour later, he rode out of St. Sebastien by the south road and dismounted. For the next hour, he strolled about in the woods to either side of the road, sometimes dragging his horse with him toward something that caught his eyes, sometimes letting the horse choose, so long as he didn't stray too far from the road.

Alert to every sound from the road, he heard a loaded cart go by toward the town, and then a carriage bowl along in the opposite direction. He saw an elderly farmer and his wife make their slow way along the road, leading a donkey laden with provisions. And not far behind them, a tall, elegant lady, walking briskly.

She wore the same warm blue pelisse he had seen already and a fetching little hat with a long blue feather. It looked vaguely familiar to him, as if he had seen it in a local shop. He didn't much care. To him, its main beauty lay in the fact that it hid none of her lovely face and very little of her shining, golden hair. She dazzled him, as she always had.

His heart soared just because she had come. And as he walked to meet her, he knew he had no control over this feeling. It simply swamped him, consumed him, and he reveled in it. *Live for the day.*

She looked a little nervous, though she walked straight to him without hesitation. "What is it? Is something wrong?"

"Not now. I just wanted to see you."

Magnificent anger flashed in her grey-green eyes. "Armand, I was worried to death! How could you send such an urgent note with no reason? I thought we were going to have to escape immediately!"

"Not immediately. Though now you mention it, are you acquainted with a smuggler called Georges?"

A hint of doubt entered her eyes. Then she said, "Yes, as it happens. At least I presume he is a smuggler. Someone who called himself Georges showed us where the Dains were hiding and sent a carriage for us."

"Is he working for the British?"

"I don't know," she said candidly. "I thought he admired Louisa."

He let out a shout of laughter, then he offered her his free arm. "Shall we walk?"

She took his arm without hesitation, and her fingers seemed to burn through her glove and his sleeves to his skin, making him more intensely aware of her than he had ever been of anyone or anything in his life before.

Side by side, with his horse following amiably enough, they strolled into the woods. It was another cold, bright autumn morning, perfect for walking, and for some time there seemed no point in saying anything.

Then, smiling up at the sky, she spoke. "Out here, there seems no urgency, no difficulty. No past or future danger. No one to judge us. It's just you and I walking."

"And kissing," he said huskily, bending to take her upturned mouth.

She allowed it, eyes closed, lips parting languidly to let him explore. It was sweet, heady. But when she nibbled at his lower lip and kissed him back, passion surged with such force, that he had to release her mouth and walk faster before he ravished her among the trees.

He wondered if she would object, and hastily banished the notion from his mind. However, it crept back at various points during those blissful couple of hours alone. In the afternoon blink of sunshine, they sat on the bank of a rushing stream and ate the bread and cheese he had brought to share with her. They talked about everything, including their past loves and griefs, childhood games, war and politics, art and literature. She was, he found, a highly educated woman, frustrated with the narrow subjects taught to young English girls.

"I avoided formal teaching a lot of the time, but I learned from my foster father's library. From just talking to him in fact."

A faint shadow crossed her face. "What a pity I will never meet him."

"Not unless you can spare the time to jaunt to Paris with me. I had a letter this morning, summoning me."

She looked down at her hands. "When do you leave?"

He shrugged. "When I can spare the time."

Amusement tugged at her lips. "You are not a very obedient foster son, are you?"

"I'm not a very obedient anything. It's why they send me on little jaunts like the one to England."

"Your forlorn hopes," she said. "Which you fulfill."

"Up to a point, mostly. But this one would have been a waste of time if you hadn't happened along."

She took his hand and lifted it to her cheek. "What are we to do, Armand?"

"Live for the day, and see where it leads."

She kissed his hand, and he kissed her lips, and she lay back against the bank in his embrace until once more lust threatened to overwhelm his good sense.

Reluctantly, he released her. "I need to go back."

"So do I," she said shakily.

He stood and reached down to help her up. "But our time isn't over. Let's ride back as far as we can."

That, too, was dangerously fun, for he took her up in the saddle in front of him and kissed her white, elegant neck while the horse walked lazily forward. Her breath quickened again, her head moving in shameless pleasure as she arched her neck under his lips.

He kicked the horse into a trot, and held her cuddled into his chest instead. It was a blissful way to travel, though when they reached the road, he had to pay a little more attention.

In the end, they managed to ride together half way back to St. Sebastien before they saw a carriage in the distance coming toward them. Hastily, he dismounted and lifted her down.

"Walk on," he said. "I'll catch you up." Still, he couldn't resist a quick kiss before he let go.

He turned the animal to make it look as though he was traveling in the opposite direction. Then, as the carriage approached, he pretended to examine the horse's hoof, brushing mud and leaves out of it.

He glanced up at the carriage as it drew alongside. It was emblazoned with St. Sebastien's coat of arms, and inside it was the mayor and his wife. Peculiarly dismayed, he lifted his hand in a cheerful wave and carried on poking at the hoof until the horse got fed up and jerked it free with a snort.

If she had recognized Isabelle– and the chances were good—she was going to feel distinctly miffed that he hadn't called that morning. Still, surely there was not much harm she could do.

# CHAPTER SEVENTEEN

"**Y**OU'RE GOING TO the fortress?" Sir Marcus said in alarm when Isabelle told him her plans over breakfast the following morning. "Is that a good idea?"

"I don't know," Isabelle admitted. "Lucie Levigne sent round a note last night asking me to join her. Apparently, it's a charitable visit to the prisoners of war who are kept there. The charity is led by the local priest, who will also be present. I think it's just a matter of taking them baskets of food and occasionally writing letters for them. Or something."

Dain still frowned. "Are you not more liable to betray yourself around victims of the enemy?"

"I don't see why, but I shall be particularly careful."

"And if you're asked to write a letter for a British prisoner, won't your excellent knowledge of English give you away?"

She shrugged. "Captain le Noir has excellent English. No one suspects him. Besides, I believe the prisoners are largely Portuguese and Spanish."

"Will he be there? Le Noir?"

"I don't know," she said honestly.

It would be a bad idea to meet him when Lucie was with her. All the same, she couldn't prevent her quickening heartbeat at the thought of even seeing him at a distance. She was like a schoolgirl in the throes of first love. And after yesterday, everything was more intense than ever. Madness…

Lucie and Father Despard arrived to collect her ten minutes later. Isabelle could see no shadow of jealousy or ill humor in the other woman's guileless face, so she had to assume that even if Lucie had seen Armand yesterday, she had not seen her. And to be fair, Isabelle had not even glanced at the carriage, but kept walking as though her mind was somewhere else entirely. It was.

They travelled in Lucie's carriage, some distance outside the town to the fortress where Armand was quartered, and where some thirty prisoners of war were incarcerated. Although Lucie chattered the whole time, at least her talk of admirers and affairs was limited by the presence of the elderly priest.

The fortress was a somewhat grim building—two buildings, in fact. The prison appeared to be the larger, before which the carriage drew up. The smaller apparently housed the officers' quarters and the offices, according to Lucie whose gaze lingered there rather too long. Deliberately, Isabelle didn't look.

As they alighted from the carriage, an officer—not Captain le Noir nor any of the men she had met before—came out of the imposing front doors to greet them. He took the baskets from Lucie's and Isabelle's hands, then summoned two soldiers to help with the rest.

Isabelle followed the officer inside, her neck prickling with the knowledge that she was inside an enemy prison. It wouldn't take too much to put her on the other side of this charitable exercise.

A group of five soldiers, apparently sergeants, were slumped in the bare hall within. Largely unshaven and tattered, they nevertheless managed to rise civilly before the French officer told them to. The baskets were laid on the long, wooden table down the center of the hall.

"For you and your men," Lucie said, smiling at them. "From St. Sebastien."

A murmur of thanks in French and Spanish rumbled from the

sergeants. The rest of the men were brought in then, and Isabelle saw that Lucie and Father Despard had the duties divided familiarly between them. Lucie, a beautiful lady bountiful, distributed the food, while the priest sat in a more private corner to allow prisoners to confess or seek spiritual guidance.

Isabelle lifted one of the baskets to help speed up the distribution process. Lucie snatched it back so speedily that Isabelle blinked. Something seemed to flash in the other woman's eyes, something very like venom, but it was so brief that it could have been a trick of the light.

Lucie's tinkling laugh sounded. "What a start you gave me! I *am* silly. I am so used to doing this alone. But yes, you deal with the baskets, and I shall ask the lieutenant about their welfare."

Lucie drifted off, and Isabelle found herself in the odd position of handing out supplies to her fellow enemies of Bonapartist France. It felt exceedingly strange and uncomfortable, not least because many of the men looked sick or harbored only partly healed injuries.

"Have you seen a doctor? A surgeon?" she asked one poor man with a dirty bandage on his arm. Some of the staining seeping out from the inside seemed to be new. But the man clearly didn't understand her, so she only smiled and wished him well.

But when the distribution was done and she looked around for Lucie to ask her about the men's medical care, the other woman was not there. Some of the prisoners had shuffled back to the depths they had come from. Others were waiting to speak to Father Despard. Isabelle approached the lieutenant who had shown them in and now stood aloof but watchful by the door.

"Monsieur, do the men have medical attention?" she asked.

"There is a surgeon among them. I suppose they don't all—excuse me, madame." He strode off to break up some dispute between the men that might otherwise have turned into a fight. He was aided, she saw, by one of the sergeants.

Feeling somewhat helpless, she decided to seek out Lucie instead. If nothing else, the mayor's wife would have access to more superior officers. *Armand*, whispered a voice in her mind, although he had never mentioned prisoners being in his charge.

The yard outside the hall was empty and silent, with no sign of Lucie.

*She has gone to Armand...* A twinge of foolish jealousy twisted through Isabelle, though she quickly thrust it aside, for she didn't really believe it. On the other hand, she didn't put it beyond Lucie to try to find him.

She followed her own curiosity, walking around the outside of the building. There were iron bars on the ground-floor windows, adding to the general grimness of the building. As she rounded the corner, a French soldier stepped out of a side door and strode off toward the back.

She hurried after him, until a hiss caught her attention and she glanced warily at the nearest window. It was open, and a hand clutched one of the iron bars.

"Madame, please," a voice said in execrable French, and then in more desperate English. "You got a kind face, missus, do me a favor, for the love of God."

His accent was not remotely Iberian, but that of London's less salubrious streets. Surprise nearly caused her to respond in English, but she managed to stop herself in time.

"What is it?" she asked in French. "What do you need?"

An unshaven, somewhat villainous face appeared, resting against the bars. "Get a letter to my wife," he pleaded.

"You want me to write it for you?" Since he looked uncomprehending at that, she made writing motions on her hand.

"Lord love you, no, ma'am, I can do that bit. Up to a point. And she can read it," he added proudly. "Trouble is, doubt they ever get to her. Never had one back, and I've been here more than a year."

Clearly encouraged by the sympathy she must have shown in her face, he added, "I got two little boys as well. I want them to hear something of their dad, know him just a bit."

His other hand came up, holding a grubby, folded paper with a name and address written on the front. He shoved it between the bars. "Take it, Madame. Give it to one of the sailors in St. Sebastien, you know?"

She stared at him, torn.

"*Le marin*," he urged in somewhat frantic French.

Her breath caught. "I understand you," she said in English and reaching up, she snatched the letter, hiding it hastily in her reticule. "I'll see that she gets it."

The prisoner smiled, revealing some broken and discolored teeth. "Bless you, madame."

He vanished from view, and Isabelle glanced furtively toward the back of the building and then the front.

Lucie Levigne stood only yards away, staring at her. "What are you doing?" she demanded.

"I promised I would send his letter home," Isabelle said calmly. She had to assume Lucie had seen her take the letter, had probably heard her speak in English. She just had to make the woman understand she had done nothing wrong.

But Lucie, all appearances to the contrary, was no fool. "How are you going to do that?"

"I shall give it to Captain le Noir," Isabelle said and walked past her, back toward the front of the building, though not before she'd caught a much more definite flash of hatred in Lucie's face.

"He has nothing to do with the prisoners, you know," Lucie said.

"But he knows the local sailors. I'm sure he'll tell me if I'm doing something wrong."

"I can tell you that."

There was a hardness in Lucie's voice Isabelle had not heard before. Jealousy… She *had* seen them together yesterday. Or perhaps she just regarded Armand, like all other men in the town, as hers for the taking. With her beauty and position, she must have had most things her own way for a long time.

And then, suddenly, she laughed and linked her arm through Isabelle's. "Well, we shall not quarrel over the poor man's letter. You have a soft heart, and I quite understand. Thank you for your help today. It gave me just the chance I needed to call on a friend we both know."

Armand again. Isabelle didn't know whether or not it was true. She just knew she didn't like the thought of any other woman being so familiar with Armand that she could visit him in his quarters. Surely, it couldn't have been the first time…

Pulling herself together, she managed to smile at Lucie, and they walked together back to the carriage where Father Despard was already waiting for them, along with the lieutenant who handed them in with great politeness. As they drove away, a few soldiers, including one officer, strode past about their business, but she saw no sign of Armand.

ARMAND WATCHED THEM go with both unease and relief. He didn't like Isabelle's presence at the prison. Nor did he like to see her with Lucie Levigne.

Knowing nothing of their charitable visit to the prisoners kept at the fortress, he had been going in search of someone to take over his duty this afternoon so that he might try and see Isabelle again. And on the front steps he had encountered the dazzlingly inappropriate vision of the mayor's wife in powder blue frills, ascending toward him.

"Madame," he said in surprise. "What on earth brings you here?"

She smiled. "My good work of the week, of course," she replied.

"And just as we both hoped, I have run into you."

"As always, you are a delight to the eyes," Armand said. "Is there someone I can fetch for you?"

She laughed and playfully slapped his hand. "Just yourself, foolish man. I do not have long, but you may take me for a walk to the garden if you wish. As a promise."

"Madame, I am on duty," he pointed out. "My time is not my own."

"And if it were?" Her husky voice and her fluttering eyelashes could no longer be ignored or brushed over. Their mild, social flirtation in no way justified this sudden escalation. Something, or someone clearly made her feel threatened or jealous, forcing her hand. Isabelle's presence.

It made him uncomfortable, but also irritated, for he had done nothing to encourage her, beyond throwing her the odd, expected compliment.

"I would take you back to your husband," he said shortly. "This is no place for a lady alone."

"I'm not alone," she said boldly, holding his gaze. "I'm with you."

"No, you're not."

She laughed, as though it were a joke, and took his arm. "Armand! I could be."

"No," he said brutally, "you couldn't. You and I can never be together, madame."

"Because of my husband?" she asked, as though amused.

"Among other things. It is time for you to go." And he strode on down the steps, leaving her alone.

It went against the chivalrous part of his nature, and he did glance back once to see her hurrying across the yard back in the direction of the prison. He swerved, walking parallel with her to be sure she was safe. Her shoulders drooped slightly. She was not used to rejection, but there was little he could do about that. If she had misunderstood his light-hearted banter, she was a lot less sophisticated than he had imagined, and he regretted it.

Especially when she did not even glance at the doorway but scuttled onward. And he saw a flash of dark blue gown vanish around the side of the building. Dear God, was Isabelle here, too?

Distinctly uneasy, now, he kept walking until he saw them together arm in arm. It caused him a pang. But there was little he could do except warn Isabelle to be wary when he could. Hastily, he ducked into the guard house, where he found Linville drinking tea and telling off a couple of soldiers.

While he cajoled for a shift-swap, he watched the mayor's carriage drive away and wondered if he was foolish to worry about something so trivial. Isabelle's position here was just too precarious…

FRUSTRATINGLY, WHEN HE called on her that afternoon, he found her in company with other town worthies, and it was almost impossible to speak to her alone.

"And how is your poor brother, Monsieur Renard?" the eldest lady asked. "I hope we will get the chance to meet him soon."

"So do I, Madame," Dain replied smoothly. His French accent was excellent, with no hint of English unless you looked for it. "Dr. Ghibert is pleased with his progress."

"And his devoted wife never leaves his side?" she pursued. "How very admirable!"

"Well, very seldom. My own wife takes her turn nursing, but my sister-in-law bears the brunt."

"As is only proper," the lady said. She clearly had more questions, but Isabelle spoke up.

"Talking of sickness, Captain le Noir, who is responsible for the health of the prisoners-of-war at the fortress?"

"I have no idea," Armand admitted. "They are not part of my responsibility."

"They need to be someone's," Isabelle retorted. "For I saw suppurating wounds and other illnesses when I visited this morning. Cannot Dr. Ghibert take a look at them?"

"I'll see what I can do," he said hastily, feeling unreasonably guilty.

At last, the wretched women went away, but Dain remained in the sitting room, glaring at him. Armand glared back.

Isabelle said, "There is an English prisoner there, too. He gave me a letter for his wife. Perhaps you know who to give it to, to make sure it reaches London?"

"Keep it," he said. "Take it yourself when you go." And suddenly the pain of parting reared its ugly head again, and he knew from the stricken look in her eyes, that she felt it, too. "The mayor's birthday reception," he said with a slightly desperate change of subject. "Are you invited?"

"We received a card of invitation," Isabelle said. "But we might use the major as an excuse to stay at home."

"I think you should go," Armand advised, for not wholly selfish reasons. "No one in the town would refuse, and it might not be good to antagonize the Levignes."

She met his gaze. "Meaning Lucie?" she asked bluntly. "She saw me take the prisoner's letter. I told her I was giving it to you. But she may have heard me speak in English a little too well. I can't make up my mind if she's suspicious of me or not."

With difficulty, Armand said to Dain, "How long before your brother can be moved?"

"I don't know. A week, maybe?"

"It may have to be sooner. But if you are still here, it would be wise to attend the mayor's reception."

Dain nodded curtly.

He had only one brief moment alone with Isabelle when she accompanied him to the front door.

"Tomorrow morning," he whispered. "Walk to the woods again. And Isabelle?"

"Yes?"

"Be careful of Lucie Levigne. She is jealous."

She met his gaze. "Does she have cause?"

"Only in her mind."

She nodded as if that was enough, and he could not resist swooping in for a kiss, though they were quickly parted by the approaching footsteps of the housekeeper from the recesses of the kitchen.

# CHAPTER EIGHTEEN

"MADAME RENARD—AT LAST!"

The mayor's birthday reception, to which everyone of note for miles around was invited, was held in the town hall. Isabelle wore her one evening gown—without Jane Verne's little diamonds—and at first glance into the hall, she felt wildly under-dressed. However, the mayor's greeting was openly admiring, so perhaps her lack of frills and jewels was taken as quiet elegance rather than insult.

"My wife has told me all about you. So delighted you could come this evening." The mayor was a floridly handsome man approaching his fifties, and grown just a little portly on too much good living. He kissed Isabelle's hand, his eyes gleaming with something more than mere admiration, something that was both avid and predatory. It was a look she had seen many times before.

"My husband, Marc Renard," she murmured, drawing her hand free to indicate Dain, standing beside her with sardonic amusement.

"Ah, monsieur, welcome!" the mayor said jovially. "You are a lucky man to possess such a wife."

"I am," Dain agreed, placing Isabelle's hand back on his arm. He smiled at Monsieur and Madame Levigne. "As are you,"

They moved on to let those following receive the mayoral welcome.

"You would appear to have another admirer," Dain murmured.

"Somewhat excessive when he has never even seen me before

tonight," Isabelle said cynically. "I think he might be getting his own back on his wife."

"For what?" asked Dain, faintly amused as he looked around the hall.

"For her rather too open favoring of Armand le Noir. Which," she added as Dain raised his eyebrows, "is all in her mind."

"Is it?" Dain murmured, his gaze fixed.

She followed it to Armand, standing with a group of other officers and ladies toward the back of the room. As though sensing their scrutiny, Armand glanced over, smiled, and raised his glass to them. Her heart skipped a beat as it always did when she saw him.

In the last couple of days, there had been other assignations, full of laughter and talk and passionate embraces. These secret meetings had only increased the bond between them. She had never been so close to anyone, and instead of being afraid of that, she loved it.

"He has no discretion," Dain murmured. "What am I supposed to do when I deign to notice his—er—favor toward you? Call him out or pursue the mayor's wife?"

"I think the former would be safer," Isabelle said wryly. "But I beg you will not."

"You may be easy on that score! But let us try to get through this evening as quietly as possible and return home intact."

She knew what he meant. This was the first large gathering they had attended, and with it came the feeling that the town was closing in around them like bind weed, making them part of its fabric from which they would struggle to escape when the time came. As come, it must. They had only to stay safe a few more days.

And in truth, the surroundings were pleasant, the hall airy and not too crowded. A small orchestra played gentle music in the back-ground, although, an acquaintance told Isabelle when she paused to greet her, there was to be dancing as well, for the younger people.

She made it sound like a treat for the children, an activity for the young, unmarried people of the town, so it came almost as a shock when the Levignes, still together, accosted Isabelle and Dain during their aimless perambulations.

"How charming to have found you both together," Lucie exclaimed.

"Is it?" Isabelle asked, amused.

"I came to ask your husband's permission," the mayor explained. "It behoves me to open the dancing part of the evening, and I would be honored if Madame Renard would be my partner."

"The honor would be ours, monsieur," Dain returned politely, although the sardonic amusement had returned to his eyes as he placed Isabelle's hand on the mayoral sleeve. "Then perhaps, Madame Levigne would grant me a similar honor?"

Madame Levigne, it seemed, was delighted to. She took Dain's arm, giving him all her attention as Isabelle, slightly bemused, was led into the center of the hall by the mayor. At the same time, people scattered to the sides, leaving them alone, while the orchestra smoothly changed its background chamber music to the much more definite, introductory strains of a waltz.

The mayor's smile was lascivious as he slid his arm around her waist and took her gloved hand in his. "Madame, your beauty quite dazzles me."

"You are too kind," she replied, following his steps.

"Not kindness, but truth," he insisted.

"I cannot believe that from a man married to my friend Lucie," Isabelle said sweetly, "who dazzles all who meet her."

"She is a delight," the mayor allowed, apparently oblivious to her set-down. "But you are something quite new to me, to the whole town, I daresay."

She raised one eyebrow. "Am I really so freakish?"

"Unique," he corrected hastily. "Your style, your elegance, even the way you speak. Madame, I am at your feet."

"That would be unfortunate on the dance floor," she observed.

The mayor blinked, and then laughed, but the exchange seemed to have set the tone for the entire dance. He made her fulsome compliments, which she turned aside or made light fun of. He allowed himself to be amused by her wit and thought of something else to say. All the while, he showed an inclination to hold her too close, which she parried by treading on his toes and apologizing for her gaucheness.

She had occasional glimpses of Dain and Lucie, sweeping past them. Lucie appeared to be employing all her arts to ensnare poor Marcus. Her eyes were wide and attentive, her lashes fluttering, her smile adoring. Was this to punish Isabelle for Armand's apparent preference?

The whole evening began to feel unreal, especially when the dance finally ended and she managed to escape the mayor's literal clutches and almost ran into Armand, only seconds before Lucie would have reached him. Lucie accosted Lieutenant Bernard instead, as though that had always been her plan. And certainly, Bernard looked ecstatic. Dain appeared to be in polite conversation with the mayor, although both pairs of eyes were on her and Armand.

"This is a mad house," Isabelle breathed as Armand presented her with a glass of wine.

"Pretty much," he agreed with a grin. "I fear you have both stumbled into a marital war. Not so much as principals but as weapons. I hope Monsieur Renard has a strong constitution and a will to resist, for I suspect the mayor is in a mood to kill. He would rather it be me, of course—or possibly Lucie—but I'm sure your husband will do at a pinch."

"I'm glad you find this so amusing!"

"Well, it *is* quite funny, especially since Lucie has not been remotely unfaithful. Or at least not with me. But take my advice and don't go anywhere unaccompanied tonight. You might pass that on to Monsieur Renard."

"Perhaps you should take your own advice," she retorted.

"Perhaps it will turn the mayor's ire—and his attentions—if *I* dance with you."

"Either that or he will hate you even more. This was meant to be a quiet evening for us. The last thing we need is the town's gossip, to say nothing of ruffled feathers among its most important citizens."

"You worry too much. Dance with me."

Despite everything, she could not resist. The secret bliss of being in his arms, of being able to talk and smile with him, overwhelmed her.

"Do you remember our dance at Audley Park?" he murmured.

"I knew you were insane by then. I think it must be catching."

"Would you really have shot me?"

She thought back to the fury, the hurt of that night as she'd finally realized what he was about. "I don't know," she said candidly. "I thought I could. I felt…used."

"There was never any question of that," he said seriously.

"I know. But now that the boot is on the other foot, as it were, you may say I was using you if and when this little masquerade is found out. I will be long gone, so you may revile me with impunity."

"I could never revile you."

Not for the first time, fear for him clawed at her stomach. "If it can save you, do it. When we began this, it never entered my head we could involve you, let alone endanger you."

"I am in no danger whatsoever," he said. "Except of loving you more every time I look at you."

Even as her heart melted, she glimpsed Lucie over his shoulder, dancing and smiling with someone else, though her gaze seemed to just slide away from Isabelle and Armand.

THE MAYOR FOUND her again at supper—a buffet from which he

offered her all the choicest morsels. She accepted only a small amount, in the hope of escaping him more quickly.

"Why, you eat like a tiny bird," the mayor said, watching avidly as she nibbled an olive.

She let it fall back onto her plate. "What a charming building this is," she said with a hint of desperation. "You must be very proud of it."

She meant the whole town must be proud, but he took it as a personal compliment. "Indeed I am. The marble hall is unique in this part of France. And as for the decoration of my official meeting room, the treasures we have on display… But come, I shall show you."

Before she could demur, he snatched her hand, all but dragging her to her feet and toward the nearby wall.

She could probably have jerked free, or even spoken sharply to force him to release her. But surrounded by people, either would have drawn the sort of attention she wished to avoid. An undignified struggle, which she had no doubt about winning, would be better undertaken in private. And if there was no privacy, then she was in no real danger of anything except accusations that she was ensnaring the mayor.

To her surprise, the ornately decorated wall opened to Levigne's touch, a private door, which swung closed to silence and gloom. A single lamp burned on the wall, casting a pale glow on a narrow staircase. Levigne released her since there was no room for them to stand side by side, and invited her to precede him.

She hesitated. There was little space for a struggle. He blocked the door. And he was no longer touching her.

"It's too dark," she said flatly.

"There are more lights at the top of the stairs." He didn't even look predatory any more, just eager to show his treasures.

She walked upstairs in front of him, and sure enough, at the top of the stairs, he lit more candles, handing her one, while he lit a lamp in the gracious passage and led her across the hall to another room.

Here, one lamp already burned, but he quickly lit others, further putting Isabelle at her ease. She duly admired the fine, painted ceiling panels, and was distracted by the glass display cabinets storing a fine collection of Chinese porcelain and ancient Egyptian jewelry.

She had bent over the cases with genuine interest when quite without warning, the mayor launched himself at her. Seizing her around the middle, he spun her around to face him and his open mouth swooped down on hers.

Sheer instinct shot her hand up between them and over her lips so that it was her palm he slobbered over. Bracing herself on the cabinet behind her, she shoved his face with all her might. His neck jerked with a somewhat ominous creak, and he staggered backward.

"That is enough, *Monsieur le Maire!*" she uttered.

But he had regained his balance, and her violence, instead angering him, seemed to inflame him. "Why, madame, you are a fiery creature! I believe I shall enjoy overcoming your reluctance."

"You won't," she said grimly as he advanced toward her. With deliberation, she withdrew a pin from her hair. "I'm leaving now, and you will not try to impede me."

The mayor laughed and kept coming. Isabelle marched toward the door, but Levigne swerved to intercept her, and then the door flew open and a man marched in.

Armand.

Levigne spun about in irritation, which was nothing to the fury that shook him when he beheld Armand.

"Ah, madame, there you are!" Armand exclaimed. "I'm afraid the town treasures must wait until next time, for your husband is looking everywhere for you."

She brushed past Levigne. "Why, what is wrong?" she demanded, only half-convinced that he was making it up.

"A message from the other Madame Renard. Her husband appears to have taken a turn for the worse."

"Oh, no. Forgive me, monsieur," she flung over her shoulder. "I wish you the happiest of birthdays, but I must go home."

She whisked out of the door, and Armand closed it firmly behind them before seizing her by the hand and running as though they were both children.

"It's a lie," he said before she could ask. "But now we need to seize your husband and depart before Levigne and Lucie compare notes."

"Lucie?"

"She's dancing with your husband again."

A breath of laughter escaped her as she flew down the massive curved staircase with him. "Oh no! You should have found a different excuse."

"What? Such *as if you don't come this instant, I'll defenestrate the mayor?*"

"At least it would have been honest."

"It would," Armand said grimly. He pulled her back at the curve. Once they turned it, they would be visible to the occupants of the hall beneath. "Dignity." He placed her hand on his arm and they descended as though they had every right to be there, worried and clearly in a hurry. "Madame's cloak, if you please," he flung at the servant at the foot of the stairs. "One moment, madame, I'll fetch your husband."

He simply strode onto the dance floor straight to Dain and Lucie. A quick bow of apology, a word to Dain, and then he was escorting them both off the floor. Isabelle, forcing herself to action before hysterical laughter took hold of her, hurried around the dance floor to meet them. A servant presented her cloak, which Armand seized while they exchanged a flurry of alarmed farewells with Lucie and then they were outside in the blessedly cold rain.

"What a bloody awful evening," Dain muttered in English as they marched across the square together. "It seems I owe you another debt, le Noir."

"No," Armand disputed. "Not if you allow me to sweep your wife off for a more pleasant evening."

Dain frowned at him in irritation. "Why would I do that? The town is clearly dangerous enough, and *you* are worse. Like it or not, I'm the only protection she has."

Although he glared at Armand, it was clear to Isabelle that he knew perfectly well he could not stop her. Nor had Armand needed to ask his permission. It was a politeness, to win his cooperation.

"No," Armand said. "I will protect her with my life."

"From yourself?" Dain asked.

"If necessary. Damn, I will take you for dinner with us if it would make you happier."

"It won't," Dain snapped and strode around the corner alone.

Isabelle blinked after him. "I think that was permission."

"No," Armand said ruefully, "that was warning. Come." He led her to the side of the square where a short row of hired carriages awaited. He called the name of an inn to the driver and handed her in.

As he landed beside her and the carriage was pulled onward, a rush of awareness struck her. The lanterns on the carriage lent a faint glow to the interior, an intimacy that was both exciting and dangerous.

It seemed to have been building for so long, this hunger, this…lust. Born of attraction and obsession and nurtured by their secret walks and embraces. His kisses. Dear God, his kisses…

The tension tightened between them. But he only took her hand and kissed it. "There is an inn just outside the town, where we can have a private room and the tastiest supper in Normandy. And then I will take you back."

She turned to search his face. "Something is wrong."

"Apart from you wandering off with the mayor, like a fly into his web?"

"I had my trusty hair pin," she retorted. "Against which no man may prevail. But yes, apart from that."

His lips quirked. "I can hide nothing from you. I thought we might enjoy this evening first."

"Before you tell me?"

He nodded.

"Tell me what?" she asked.

He sighed. "That I have been summoned to Paris, by military authority this time. I have to go."

Her throat constricted. "When?"

"I can stretch it to the day after tomorrow if I ride like the wind." His fingers tightened. "You might want to consider leaving shortly after that. My men will come with me, and I don't like to leave you here without protection. You have a way back?"

She nodded, unable to speak. It was all coming to an end, her idyll of love. The feeling was real, the rest mere fantasy.

He touched her cheek. "Don't look like that," he said softly. "Let us enjoy the last of our time together."

She smiled a little shakily. "Distraction?"

"Actually, I think this time Paris is the distraction. Look, we are here."

He handed her down, paid the driver, and led her inside.

The innkeeper greeted him by name and with great delight, ushering them at once into the private supper room he asked for. A cozy fire burned in the grate and a table sat before it. The innkeeper bustled away to fetch wine and order their supper.

"How many other women have you brought here?" Isabelle wondered aloud as he removed her cloak and hung it on the stand by the door.

"None," he said, clearly surprised, though whether at her question or his answer was moot. "I've had a few convivial evenings with my fellow officers, no more or less." He came and pulled out a chair for her, then sat in the one at right-angles to hers. A smile flickered across his lips. "There have been other inns, other women. I have never been an angel. Since I met you, no other woman interests me. There is only you."

"Why?" she whispered.

He shook his head. "I don't know. Why me?"

"I don't know," she repeated. "I can think of all the reasons I like you. That you make me laugh, that I never know what you will say or do next, that you are quick-witted and loyal and interesting, strong and handsome... The love comes from something deeper, something I cannot explain. It is as if we are bound, you and I."

He took her hand, pressing it to his lips. "That is what I feel," he said hoarsely. "What I have always felt."

She reached up to cup his rough cheek, then let it fall as their wine was brought in.

It was a wonderful evening, as he had promised. Excellent food and drink combined with fun and laughter and the glow of acknowledged love.

"Does it bring back memories?" he asked once. "The speech, the tastes and smells of France?"

"Not really memories, since I left when I was so young. It is more like...echoes, elusive familiarities that I cannot trace to anything definite."

"But you like being in France?"

Her smile faded. "This isn't being in France. St. Sebastien is like an isolated outpost, my life here one of pretense that could end in disaster at any moment. It isn't real."

He searched her face. "Am I not real?"

She laid her head on his shoulder. "Only you are real."

He banished her pain with a kiss, and then pastries were brought in along with a sweet, thick wine that threatened to go to her head.

She could have stayed there with him all night.

"Shall we go?" he said at last, and her heart thundered.

They need not go. The night could be spent here with him, a night of love such as she had never known. A night to seal their bond.

And their inevitable farewell.

"Yes," she got out. "We should go."

And he stood and fetched her cloak, placing it delicately around her shoulders.

Somehow, there was a hired carriage waiting to take them back to town. And this time as they drove through the darkness, close together on the seat, their fingers linked, there was a sort of desperation to the intimacy.

He handed her down in the Rue l'Église and paid off the driver before escorting her to the door.

"I'll come in if I may," he said abruptly, "and speak to…your husband."

The darkness could be hiding anyone, she supposed as she opened the door with her key and walked inside.

The house was silent, although a lamp burned in the hall and another in the sitting room. Which was empty.

"I think he might have gone to bed," she said, nervous for some reason she couldn't grasp. She had been alone with him for most of the evening, after all. "Would you like a brandy while we wait and see if he comes back?"

She poured it and brought it to him on the sofa. He caught her hand, drawing her down beside him.

"We do not need to part," he said with unusual difficulty. He took a gulp of the brandy, then met her gaze. "There is a way for us to be together. Come with me to Paris."

Her breath caught. Her heart leapt. But that, too, was fantasy. "I can't. I can't leave the Dains here alone."

"Then come when they are gone."

"How can I? You will probably already have left on some other commission."

He almost threw the glass on to the table beside him. "Which is the greater madness?" he demanded. "For us to live apart? Or for us to be together?"

"There has always been more than us to consider." She clung to his hand. "You could come with me, Armand. Torbridge would make it right, welcome you with open arms. You need betray nothing and no one. By the time he realizes it—"

"Stop it," Armand said violently. "I would still be a traitor. *I* would know it. You would know it. It will never happen. I will never leave France. You had no choice in leaving. You were a child and your parents' lives were in danger. This is a different France now, where you would not be the enemy. England is not your home, Isabelle."

"It is the only home I've known. And I can make my way there. I always have."

"You could make your way here."

"Sitting alone waiting for you? I have had enough of sitting at home waiting for a husband."

As soon as the words were out, she regretted them. She bit her lip, but they could not be taken back. Only explained. "I do not mean—"

"You would compare me to *him*?" he interrupted. "After everything, it comes down to that?" He sprang to his feet, almost tearing his hand from hers so that he could pace angrily up and down the room that was too small to hold him.

He threw back his head. "You are right. Damn it, you are right. It is impossible. I will not go and you will not stay. There is nothing for us but memory. Except, perhaps, the end of the war. Goodbye, Isabelle, my sweet love."

He had called her that once before, in mockery when he had first come across her here. There was no mockery now, only pain, but before she could realize it properly, he had scooped her up into his arms, crushing her mouth beneath his in a hard, passionate kiss that melted her bones. With a sob, she flung her arms around his neck and kissed him back.

At last, he wrenched his mouth free, almost throwing her from him so that she stumbled back onto the sofa. He stormed out of the room before she could speak, before she could rise and take more than a step after him. From instinct, she ran, but the front door opened and closed, leaving nothing but a blast of cold air where he had been.

Just like that, he was gone.

And her life crumbled.

She leaned against the front door before her legs refused to support her. She could not even hear his footsteps. He had run from her.

It was over.

*It's for the best. We will both recover. It's for the best.*

*No, it isn't.*

She became aware of dampness on her face and wiped the tears aside. They would help no one.

Something scratched the other side of the door. Her heart seemed to stop.

Her mouth dry, she lifted the latch, opened it a crack, and then wide.

Armand stepped over the threshold, staring at her as she closed the door once more. He opened his mouth, but she pressed her fingers to his lips. Then she took his hand, and in silence, led him to the stairs.

# CHAPTER NINETEEN

THEY DIDN'T SPEAK until she closed the bedchamber door and turned to face him. She was trembling.

"I'm sorry," he whispered. "My damnable temper. I will not waste this time with you, if you agree to share it with me."

"Would I have brought you here to rail at you and send you away?" she managed.

He reached out and took her hand. His was not quite steady either. "I never know what you will say or do. It's one of the reasons I like you."

"Just like?"

His lips curved. "I thought we were already agreed that the love is something else entirely." He stepped closer and cupped her face between his hands. "I have wanted this since the first moment I saw you."

"So have I," she confessed, and his smiling mouth came down on hers, slow and gentle and unspeakably tender.

Somehow, she had expected more urgency, more demanding haste. But his seduction was soft and exquisite, every caress of hands and lips sweeter than the last. He undressed her with such care that she might have doubted his passion had she not looked into his clouded, dark eyes and read there every wild lust she could have imagined and a few she could not. The combination of that untamed desire and the gentleness of his touch almost undid her.

She moaned, pushing his shirt off his shoulders and kissing his chest, his shoulders, his throat. She had never been so aroused in her life. And they had barely begun.

When she stood before him naked and he touched the tip of his tongue to her nipple, her knees gave way. He caught her and carried her to the bed, where he laid her as if she were priceless porcelain that might break at any moment. When he kicked off his loosened pantaloons and underclothes, she could not breathe. Her arms lifted for him, desperate to touch, to hold. And he came to her, worshiping her body from head to toe, his tender fingers ever bolder as they reached her most intimate places, playing her like a musical instrument.

Lost in him, in wonder, she absorbed every instant of growing bliss, loving him with her lips and hands until his breath came faster than hers, and he smiled as he entered her body and took her the rest of the way to the most intense ecstasy she had ever known.

She wept with joy when he reached his own pleasure in her. Though he left his seed outside her body, and that made the tears come harder.

"God, I love you," he whispered, kissing the dampness from her face. "Tell me that is joy and not regret."

"You know it is."

He smiled and kissed her, and they both closed their eyes and slept.

ARMAND WOKE TO movement in the house, and the realization he was curled around a softly feminine, warm, naked body. Remembering where he was and what he had finally done, intense happiness soared up from his toes, even before he opened his eyes to the sweet curve of her cheek and the wild mass of her beautiful, golden hair.

After a moment, he eased himself up on one elbow and watched her as she slept. Her loveliness made him ache. For she was both his and not his.

They had today, tonight if she would have him again, and then he would have to bolt to Paris, leaving her alone here. Before then, he must speak to Dain, encourage him to go as soon as they were able. Such as tomorrow night.

She stirred, sighed, and they smiled together while she stretched luxuriously. Armand's lust, already at morning attention, consumed him. He loomed over her, and she came into his arms with such eagerness that he took her at once. As if to make up for last night's delicate seduction, this lovemaking was urgent and wild, as if they had both agreed to it. Certainly, it swept them both along like an unstoppable tide, and leaving her body in time felt like the most heroic act of his life.

When he could speak, he whispered in her ear, "Shall I climb out of the window?"

A breath of laughter shook her. "No," she said and kissed his chest. "You will breakfast with us."

They shared the washing water. He helped her with her laces. She brushed down his uniform. The intimacy, a hint of how things would be were they together, caused him both delight and pain. Like children, they listened at the bedchamber door, crept along the passage past the other bedchambers, and fled downstairs. They hid behind coats as Madame Vosges hurried toward the kitchen.

Then Isabelle reached for the front door, and he thought she was ejecting him after all, But she only closed it again with a decided snap, smiled at him, and led him across the hall to the dining room.

"Captain le Noir is joining is for breakfast," she said boldly.

Mrs. Dain, both alarmed and surprised, eyed him warily as though he had come to arrest them. Sir Marcus Dain frowned for quite other reasons, as though he knew full well Armand had not just arrived. But there was no jealousy about him. The man was trying to protect a friend, a motive Armand respected absolutely. But last night… Quite aside from the beauty and pleasure of what they'd shared, last night had been *necessary* to them both, and he would never regret it.

"I've been called to Paris," he told Dain abruptly while spreading butter on his freshly baked bread. "I'll have to leave at first light tomorrow morning. And I think you should seriously consider leaving tomorrow night, or the night after at the latest."

"Why?" Dain asked.

"I will not be here to watch your backs. And with the best will in the world, you are not blending into the town. You are making enemies."

"Who?" Dain demanded.

"The mayor and his wife."

Dain blinked. "Because Isabelle would not succumb to his charms? While I was at the same party?"

"And because you would not succumb to hers. To Lucie Levigne it is clear only that, like me, you prefer Isabelle to her."

Dain scowled. "Why can they not simply prefer each other?"

"It would be simplest," Armand agree, "but it is not so. By their own lights, we have all insulted them, and neither takes kindly to that. I have my own protection, there is little they can do to harm me without harming themselves. But you are vulnerable to any kind of accusation they might make, any inquiry sent to Paris. You should be gone before they receive any reply. Tomorrow night at the latest, sir. Promise me."

Dain exchanged glances with his sister-in-law and Isabelle, before returning his gaze to Armand. "I will try. My brother is much better. He can even walk with crutches, although getting him to the beach and into the boat may be problematic. I'm not sure I can carry him alone."

"Get him to the path," Armand instructed. "Georges will see that he's helped."

"How can you be sure?"

"Because I'll arrest him if he doesn't," Armand said flatly. He took a gulp of coffee. "If you go tonight, I will help you."

Again, Dain glanced at his sister-in-law.

"Tomorrow would be better," she said firmly. "One more day will make a big difference to him."

"Then make it tomorrow." He set down his cup. "I have today as leave, to prepare for my journey. Which I can do in an hour." He looked at Isabelle and smiled. "I would like to spend this day with you."

When she smiled back, his heart melted.

"Is this wise?" Dain said abruptly. "Are you not simply making your parting harder?"

"It couldn't be harder," Armand said frankly. "I am trying to make it bearable."

HALFWAY THROUGH THEIR last day together, it began to rain, but Armand refused to let it spoil or even curtail their fun. With the horse blanket over their heads, they walked in the woods and sang loudly.

As their song ended in laughter, the question spilled from his lips. "Will you marry me, Isabelle?"

She stared at him, the smile still trembling on her lips. The light in her eyes was soft and warm. She reached up to his damp cheek. "Of course, I will. As soon as the war is over." She kissed him, like a promise.

The wet blanket slid from their hold to the ground, and rain ran down their faces and into their mouths. But they both smiled.

"We can write to each other," he said, just a little desperately. "The smugglers will deliver for us. Some of the time."

"There will be a way," she agreed. "If we don't give up. Armand, is there no shelter hereabout?"

"Of course there is. It's only half a mile to the inn."

They dried off before the inn's roaring fire and ate a warm meal. By the time they had finished, the rain was off, but the sun was low in the sky and the knowledge that their day was almost over lay heavily on both their hearts.

As before, they rode together on his horse most of the way back to St. Sebastien. Then they dismounted and walked together to the Rue l'Église, where, he was amused to see curtains twitching. Were the Renards' neighbors really so interested in their affair of the heart?

No, he realized with a sudden plunge of his stomach. They were interested in the soldiers milling in and out of the Renards' house.

"Oh, dear God," Isabelle whispered. As one, they sped forward.

Armand didn't even try to tie his horse to the garden fence. He simply strode up the path, roaring, "What the devil is going on here?"

The two soldiers at the door shot to attention.

"Searching, sir. There's been an accusation."

"Of what?" Armand demanded. "By whom?"

"I don't know, Captain," the soldier said desperately. "We're just following orders."

"Bah!" Whipping up his rage to drown the terror, he flung himself into the house, Isabelle at his heels.

Sir Marcus Dain stood in the hall, his mouth rigid, his hands tied behind his back. Furiously, Armand drew his sword, and Dain's eyes widened in disbelief. Armand would have laughed if he hadn't been so angry. With one slash, he cut through the ropes that bound the Englishman.

"Who is in charge here?" he yelled. "Show your damned face!"

Lieutenant Bernard's hopeful countenance appeared over the bannister. "I am, Captain."

"Told you he wouldn't like it," Caron said laconically.

For the first time, Armand noticed him and Boucher lounging in the sitting room doorway. Boucher was picking his teeth. Clearly, neither were helping.

"Then why the devil didn't you stop it?" Armand demanded.

"He's the lieutenant," Caron pointed out.

"Lieutenant, take your men and get out!"

"But, Captain—"

"Don't you know who these people are? Friends of the mayor himself, with connections that reach all the way to the emperor." He leapt up the stairs, three at a time. "Out!" he roared, shoving soldiers toward the stairs, dragging one out of Major Dain's bedchamber with particular violence. "How dare you? That man was injured severely in the service of his country, while you imbeciles laze around picking over his possessions. By God, there will be court martials over this day!"

There probably would, he reflected. His.

But somehow, with the cooperation of Boucher and Caron who recited all the dire things likely to happen after such a fiasco as this, he marched all the soldiers outside, sent them back to barracks, and slammed the door on them.

"Thank you, sir," whispered Mrs. Dain from the stairs.

"Is your husband well?" Armand asked curtly.

She nodded.

Armand swept his gaze around the household. "Then prepare. You have to leave tonight."

"How?" Isabelle asked intensely as they sat on the rocks by the beach where they had arrived only a week ago. Shadows moved in the darkness, going about the purely business part of the night. "How could this happen so quickly?"

"The accusation came from the mayor," Armand said. "A suspicion of smuggling activities. Probably, he was goaded or at least encouraged by Lucie. But they both knew my commission here, and they both knew I had leave today before departing tomorrow. They knew they could bully my lieutenant into doing their bidding when I was not there. For one thing, Bernard is putty in Lucie's hands. At the same time, I'm still nominally in charge, so I am responsible for the fiasco when a supposedly important family is troubled for nothing."

Isabelle shook her head. "No, Lucie thought there would be something to find. That day, with the prisoners...she suspects me. She hoped for my arrest."

Armand shrugged. "Whatever the results, they win. At the very least, you are inconvenienced, and I get my wrists slapped."

She turned to him, a look of fear in her eyes. Throughout everything, their adventures in England and here in France, she had never been this frightened for him before. "Won't it be worse than slapped wrists? You stopped them searching and arresting us, and when we disappear... If the truth comes out that you helped us—"

"Why should it?" he interrupted. He smiled, even nudged her as though they were children sitting on a wall and bantering. "In any case, I have friends in high places."

She threaded her fingers with his in the darkness. "Come with us, Armand," she pleaded.

"I can't. You know I can't."

"It might be sensible," Dain said from the darkness.

"Not to me."

"Torbridge will speak for you," Dain said. "As will I."

"I like your friend Torbridge," Armand said. "God knows why. But I'll be damned if I hand my life over to him. In any case..." He shrugged. "This is France. This is home."

Isabelle turned her head to him once more, staring. Her fingers tightened on his. Something tugged at her, elusive, important, but out of reach.

"Very soon now," she whispered, "you're going to need more distraction."

His fingers twisted, caressing hers. "No."

"No?" she repeated with twinge of pain. She supposed their relationship was too new, that he felt it less deeply than she did.

"It's odd," he murmured, thoughtfully, as Dain fell into low conversation with his brother. "Now that we're about to part, I seem to see everything, see myself, with new clarity. My constant search for distraction from my grief had become an end in itself. Even the grief for Rose and my son had become twisted, almost a crutch to hold on to, a reason for all my diversions, to give significance to a life that has become empty of real meaning, real ambition."

He kicked the sand, as if he could not be still, but would not move from her side.

"This endless war for its own sake," he said violently, "for an emperor in whom I no longer believe… It has become pointless to me. And so, I lived in a constant cycle of distraction to stop myself thinking and *feeling*."

He turned his head to her and his teeth gleamed in a flash of some half-covered, shifting lantern. "And then there was you, dazzling my darkness, my finest distraction ever. I have no idea how or when you became more than that, but I suspected we were still in England at the time."

Isabelle pressed her hand to her too-full heart. As the gladness seeped in among the ache, she tried to smile back.

"I will always mourn my lost family," he said softly, "always miss them. But you—" He broke off with a soft laugh and swung her hand high. "You challenged me, cajoled, and seduced me back to life."

"I'm glad," she whispered as he kissed her hand.

"Rose would have liked you," he said abruptly.

She leaned into him, almost at peace. Then she said lightly, "Pierre would *not* have liked you. That is all in our favor."

Armand grinned, but his gaze seemed to have moved beyond her, to not one winking light but three or four.

"Georges," he said urgently. "Are there more of you to come?"

"No. We're ready to go. We just need to get the passengers..." Georges broke off, swearing as he took a step past Armand, also staring at the lights. "It's soldiers!" He turned urgently back to his own shadowy accomplices. "Go! Now!"

Isabelle jumped up in alarm. The boats were already moving, one being heaved into the water, but on Georges's command, the smugglers pushed harder and threw themselves in beside their cargo.

In panic, Georges, seized Louisa Dain by the arm, tugging her toward the other boat. "Hurry! We need to go!"

"Wait!" Isabelle hissed. "You must help the major! We are right behind you. Armand, run for God's sake, before they see you."

"There's no time," Armand said with strange calmness. "Stay where you are Georges. Allow the lady some dignity."

"Dignity be damned!" Dain exclaimed, shoving past him none too gently. "If you won't help, get out of our way!"

But the soldiers were running across the beach. One paused, raising his rile at the boat already on the glassy sea. The others slowed, raising their weapons and both Dain and Georges halted uncertainly, looking wildly around them for escape.

Isabelle stepped in front of Armand, pushing him to run while he could. His hat was off, so they might not realize he was a soldier, too. Their captain, in fact.

But she should have known Armand would never take the easy way out, not when it would leave her to be arrested. On the other hand, if he was arrested, too...

He swerved past her, marching straight in front of the soldiers' guns. "What the devil are you about now?" he demanded.

The soldier in front raised his lantern, and Isabelle saw the same officer as had led the search of the house that afternoon. Lieutenant Bernard. "Bring the lights!" he snapped.

"Captain?" one of the men said in amazement when the glow spread around everyone. The men began to lower their rifles.

"What are *you* about now?" Lieutenant Bernard sneered. "Men, keep your rifles aimed."

The men looked at each other. A couple of them raised their rifles again in a half-hearted way. But, with relief, Isabelle saw that none of them, even the one who'd been aiming at the vanishing boat, were likely to use them now.

"Important business that you are about to wreck!" Armand fumed. "Twice in one day. Even for you, Bernard, that is a record! You have seen nothing here and must return to the barracks."

"While you send these English people, including your lover, back home? There is a word for men like you."

"There is a word for men like you, too," Armand retorted. "And I'm not so mealy-mouthed as you about saying it! Cretin!"

Lieutenant Bernard started forward in fury. Armand placed his palm on the man's chest and shoved him backward, hard. The lieutenant flew at him, but Armand was quicker. He side-stepped and grabbed his underling, twisting his arm up his back.

The soldiers lowered their rifles with relief. It was only the captain they would obey.

"Listen carefully," Armand hissed. "Madam Renard is not English, she's as French as you and me and considerably braver. She goes to England with the blessing of...well those close to the emperor. To work for us. Do you understand? Her information will be invaluable—certainly a lot more valuable to France than your foolish bumbling after smugglers. You already know this man," he waved one hand at Georges, "is working for us!"

Isabelle tried not to blink at this. Georges, she thought, worked for everyone.

"I don't believe you!" the lieutenant panted.

"Imbecile! Why else would I be here? And incidentally, I don't believe our superiors would think highly of *you* arresting *me* on the word of a jealous woman you want to bed!"

Lieutenant Bernard stopped struggling.

"I thought so," Armand said grimly and released him.

The lieutenant shook himself. "You should have told me what you were doing," he muttered.

"I had reservations about trusting you with such secrets. Justified, it seems by today's events. Now, march the men back to the west beach, and I'll speak to you before I leave for Paris. It seems I will *have* to trust you, now. Don't let me down."

A hundred expressions passed across the lieutenant's face, including chagrin, doubt, and suspicion, and yet overlaying all, a faint hope, surely, of earning the trust Armand almost offered. He straightened. "Yes, Captain. Men, about face and march!"

Georges and the Dains were gazing at Armand in a bizarre mixture of astonishment and admiration. Isabelle knew how they felt, but other emotions, other knowledge was overwhelming her now as those elusive threads of realization began to come together in understanding at last.

"Now you are implicated without doubt," Dain said urgently. "You must come with us or you will die."

"He's right," Georges said. "I can take you, too. We'll catch up with the ship just beyond the headland."

Armand laughed. "I thank you for your concern, but it's quite unwarranted. I'm off to Paris, and no one will touch me."

The major, balanced between his wife and brother said, "Knock him on the head. Just bring him."

Armand grinned at him and offered his hand. "Au revoir, my friend. When the war is over, we'll meet again. Madame. Sir." He shook hands formally with all of them, then gently took Louisa's place and helped Dain carry the major to the boat. Georges lifted Louisa in, and Dain clambered up after her.

Armand turned to Isabelle, and she thought her heart would burst. In front of everyone, he put his arms around her and tipped up her head. "No words. Just remember. And soon, I will come for you."

"No." She clung to his wrist, watching the pain and confusion flit across his face. She smiled shakily, "There will be no need, for I'll already be with you. I'm staying."

"You can't!" Louisa exclaimed from her position, fussing over her husband.

"I can. I must. Don't you see? Home isn't a particular piece of land. It isn't determined by which side of the sea you were born, or who your family is. Home is with the people you love, and I love Armand more than my life. Where he is, is my home. Here, take this, Marcus." She thrust the prisoner's letter into Dain's hand. "See it reaches its destination for me."

Dain took it wordlessly. For an instant, everyone stared at her, more than half-appalled. Then Armand swept her up, crushing her mouth under his and striding back up the beach. Half-laughing through the kiss, she waved over his shoulder at the retreating boat.

Armand set her back on her feet, and together they watched the vessel and its occupants vanish into the darkness.

"Are you sure?" he asked hoarsely.

"I think it's the only thing I've ever been sure about in my whole life."

He hugged her to his side, for once lost for words.

Her position was precarious, she had thrown in everything with the man at her side in what was, effectively, a strange country, whose government had been her enemy all her life. And yet, intense happiness settled over her, sweeping her up in hope and excitement and wonder.

A new life. A new home.

# CHAPTER TWENTY

ISABELLE STOOD AT the open window of the Paris *pension*, gazing down at the bustling street below. Pedestrians of all kinds mingled with carriages and street vendors. Delicious cooking smells drifted up to her, making her stomach rumble, even among occasional whiffs of more noxious city odors.

Between the buildings opposite, she glimpsed the River Seine. Armand had promised to accompany her for a walk along its banks, as soon as he returned.

They had ridden at breakneck speed from St. Sebastien, parting soon from the familiar faces of Boucher, Caron, Dupont, and Lefevre who followed more slowly without changing horses every few miles. It had made an exhausting journey, but an exciting, even delightful one because it had been taken with Armand.

Having tumbled into this *pension*, with which Armand was clearly familiar, she had slept like the dead. But Armand had risen at first light, kissed her goodbye, and gone off to answer his general's summons, leaving Isabelle to sleep longer.

However, curiosity had got the better of her. She could not stay in bed when she was in Paris. As long as her parents had been alive, they had dreamed of returning here, more even than to their lost estates in southern France. And quite unexpectedly, she was *here*.

And she did not think she could wait for Armand. Closing the window, she swept up her cloak and swung it around her shoulders.

Then she reached for her bonnet.

And a knock sounded at the door.

She straightened, suddenly wary, for Armand would not knock. But she was being silly. It would be Madame Rievaulx, their landlady. "*Entrez*," she said calmly.

The door opened and a gentleman strolled in. Tall and slender, he walked with a decided limp that detracted nothing from his sheer presence. He carried himself with the pride of an aristocrat and the unconscious confidence that Isabelle associated with power.

As his gaze fell on her, he paused for an instant before closing the door behind him. He removed his hat but inclined his head rather than bowed. "Mademoiselle?"

"Madame," she corrected. "How might I help you?"

His gaze took in the apartment, which served as both sitting room and bedchamber. "You could point me in the direction of Captain le Noir."

"He is not here. If you leave your card, I will see he receives it."

The gentleman's eyes came back to her, and she was almost frightened. They were cool, assessing, formidably intelligent, at once perceptive and dismissive. Their power took her breath away. He smiled gently. "I will wait. Don't let me keep you,"

"I wouldn't dream of it. But you will not wait here."

The hooded eyelids came down and rose. He seemed faintly amused. "I will not?"

"You will not." There was something undeniably intimidating, almost sinister about her guest, and she would not allow him to remain here, neither alone with her nor without her.

His lips curved into a faint, cold smile. "I believe we have a misunderstanding. And my manners are at fault. You are...?"

"Isabelle de Renarde," said Armand from the doorway.

Both Isabelle and her visitor swung at once to face him. Her heart skipped a beat because he looked so handsome and smart in his uniform, a faint smile playing around his lips. But there was defiance in his eyes as well as a hint of irritation. She had been so focused on the somewhat alarming caller that she hadn't even heard the door open.

He kicked it closed with his heel and walked into the room to stand beside Isabelle, facing the sinister stranger. "My betrothed."

One elegant eyebrow lifted. "Indeed. Felicitations, dear boy. Am I now worthy of a more proper greeting?"

To her surprise, Armand's face relaxed. He took a step nearer their visitor and the two men embraced.

Understanding began to dawn on Isabelle, and with it came guilt over her quick dismissal of the caller. "Oh! Is *this* your Abbé T?"

"It is," Armand said, releasing him and scowling. "And if you knew him better, you would not be surprised that my general had nothing to say to me. His summons, I believe, was at *your* behest."

The abbé shrugged. "Well, you would not obey my summonses, which I have been issuing since you returned from England. I trust it is not going to become one of your grudges?"

"I don't bear grudges," Armand said at once, "and in any case, it isn't. In fact, I'm very glad to see you, because we need your help."

The abbé sighed. "It is as well I am not easily offended. What do you want of me?"

"Isabelle was an émigré in England," Armand said bluntly. "Basically, we need to establish her right to be here so we can be married."

The abbé regarded her, not without interest. "Who were your family?"

She lifted her chin. "De Brantome."

The piercing eyes seemed to go straight through her. He smiled faintly. "I believe I knew your uncle, the Duc de Moneau."

"You did?" she said, startled.

"I am only surprised you choose to ally yourself with this low-born oaf, for contrary to popular belief, he is not my son, natural or otherwise. I only took an interest in him because for some reason, I liked him. Mostly, I can't understand that either."

"Yes, you can," Isabelle said shrewdly, and for an instant, genuine amusement twinkled in the abbé's eyes.

"I believe I shall like you, too. Very well, I shall arrange everything that is necessary. When do you wish to be married?"

"As soon as possible," Armand replied.

The abbé eased himself into the chair by the fire and stretched out his bad leg. He tapped his finger against his lips, glancing from her to Armand and back. "Very well. This afternoon will do. I had set it aside for Armand in any case. And you and I, my dear, will need to have a long talk. Very soon."

"About what?" she said, bewildered.

"Great Britain," the abbé replied, still watching her very carefully.

"You're wrong," Armand said amiably, mystifying Isabelle thoroughly. "She has nothing to do with you. She doesn't even know who you are."

A frown tugged at her brow. "Who *are* you?" she asked.

Armand sighed. "Allow me to present to you Prince Charles Maurice de Talleyrand-Perigord."

The blood sang in her ears. This was the "defrocked priest" Armand had claimed was his foster father. This aristocratic churchman turned revolutionary, who had not only survived but thrived during the countless changes of regime in France since the revolution. A clever diplomat and puller of strings, the master of a massive network of information. And a man who had both supported and betrayed Bonaparte, according to rumor. But it wasn't the fact that he carried such power that floored her.

It was the realization that Torbridge had known all along. In defecting to France with Armand, she had put herself just where he had always wanted her. Next to Talleyrand.

The great man smiled in understanding. "I don't suppose you know a man called Lord Torbridge?"

"Even I know Torbridge," Armand scoffed.

"Which is precisely why I summoned you," Talleyrand said.

"WE HAVE BEEN manipulated from the beginning!" Isabelle raged when Talleyrand had finally left them alone. She paced the room much more in Armand's style than her own. "I for one will not play the spy or the traitor, not for either of them!"

"I'm not sure that is what's wanted of either of us," Armand said thoughtfully, sitting on the bed and watching her.

She swung on him. "Is that why you were so suspicious of me when we first met in France? You thought I was pursuing you? To get to your foster-father?"

"It crossed my mind," he admitted. "I thought of you as my untouchable, unattainable angel, and for a short while—a very short while—you seemed...sullied. I'm sorry. It was soon perfectly clear you had no idea about my background. Though I doubted Torbridge was so ignorant."

"I wish you had warned me."

"Why?" He caught her hand as she strode past him and pulled her onto the bed beside him. "Would it have made any difference? If you had known my abbé was Talleyrand, would you have gone back to England with the Dains?"

She shook her head. "No. No, you know I would not. Unless it was to slap Torbridge's devious face before I came home again."

Armand smiled and drew her back to lie with him on the bed. "Home. You called France home."

She let herself relax into his arms. "*You* are home."

"Then don't be angry. Don't regret Torbridge, because he sent you to me. Don't regret Talleyrand, because despite everything, I love him. And between them, they have brought us together."

She touched his cheek. "That is true."

He kissed her. "You might also consider that it is not betrayal either of them want from you or me, but a way to peace. The emperor's failure in Russia weakens him, leaves him open to negotiation at the very least. Perhaps we have an honorable part to play in what follows."

"Perhaps," she agreed, doubtful but intrigued.

He kissed her again, with just a little more urgency in his persuasive lips. "In the meantime, we have just over three hours until you marry this unmarriable soldier. How would you like to spend it?"

She smiled against his lips. "Walking by the Seine."

"And?" His hands swept down her body, making her gasp and arch into his caress.

"And this," she whispered.

"Do you love me?" he asked fiercely.

She threw both arms around his neck. "With all my heart."

# EPILOGUE

AS HIS COACH thundered through the village of Carmillac, Armand threw himself forward to stare out of the window. The sudden intensification of pain made him tug in frustration at the bandage around his head. Despite the surgeon's instructions to remain calm and relaxed as much as possible, he could not. He yearned to be home too badly, for Isabelle should be delivering their first child any day, and he had no idea how either of them fared. Fear for them, at this most dangerous time of a woman's life, ate him up.

How ironic it would be for him to have survived this head wound received in battle at Dresden only to discover he had lost everything that made his life worthwhile... But he would not, *could* not think of such a possibility.

There was nothing to distract him but scenery as they sped out of the village and onward down the hedge-lined road. Abbe T had given them the farmhouse as a wedding present. It was small enough not to draw undue attention, large enough to entertain friends and family. Even a cousin of Isabelle's had come to stay for a week, while he had had opportunity during his last leave of absence, to introduce her to several of his closest friends. It had warmed his heart to see her welcome them, and appreciate them as he did.

But this child, which he both longed for and feared for the danger it presented to Isabelle... He rubbed his head through the bandage, and sat at the very edge of the seat, drumming his fingers against the window. The coach swerved to the left, slowing on the narrower track that led to the farm.

His heart drumming, he barely waited for the coach to halt before he jumped out. That didn't help his headache, either, but he could not wait. The front door was open, while a maid swept the step.

"Monsieur!" she exclaimed, scrambling to her feet in apparent delight.

Somewhere that surprised him, but he had no time to dwell on anything other than Isabelle. "Where is my wife?" he demanded.

"In the garden, monsieur, with—"

He pushed past her, charging through the house to the side door that led to the garden and bolted outside, where he came to a sudden, dizzying stop.

The September air was warm, yet fresh and sweet. He realized it smelled of home. Every sense spoke of home here, not least the image of Isabelle, hatless in the sunshine, stretched out on a blanket on the grass, bent over whatever was hidden in the shade of a parasol.

His wife was smiling, her eyes soft and tender as she gazed down at the object of her attention. She was so beautiful he could not breathe, so alive that he wanted to shout and weep for joy.

Then she looked up, and his heart stood still.

Her hand flew to her breast. For an instant, the smile seemed frozen to her face, and then with a sob, she leapt to her feet and flew to him. He caught her in his arms and her fingers were on his face.

"Oh, my love, my love, you are hurt," she whispered, touching his bandage. "What..." The rest was lost as he kissed her. She returned the embrace with enthusiasm.

After a few moments, his mind began to work again. He recognized the bump had gone from her belly and began to suspect what he should always have known, what—indeed who—lay beneath the parasol.

With a gasp, he tore his lips free.

"I'm fine," he said hoarsely. "Well on the mend. And you, you are well?"

"More than well," she whispered, tugging his hand to make him move his apparently paralyzed feet. "Come."

And there beneath the parasol lay the tiniest, most perfect being in the world. A baby.

"Your daughter," Isabelle said. "I named her Aimée."

"Perfect," he whispered, dropping to his knees on the blanket. He touched his daughter's cheek with the tip of his little finger. She took a swipe at it and caught it, holding on with a strength that made him smile. "Oh, my dear, aren't you clever?"

"Aimée?" she asked shakily. "Or me?"

He lifted the baby in one arm, and with the other, drew Isabelle close in to his side. "Both. I am the luckiest man alive."

She leaned in to him. "How long can you stay?"

"Two months or more, the surgeon said."

"Tell me everything," she said anxiously.

"After you've told me everything," he insisted. "And kiss me again."

She obeyed the latter instruction, then rested her head on his shoulder. "I have a family of my own. I never knew, never imagined, I could be so happy as now, when I have you both together." She smiled. "I wonder what is happening at the Hart Inn right now. I wonder if Lily married her farmer or held out for true love."

"That is another story. At the moment, I am more than contented with mine." He kissed her and then his daughter.

"So am I," Isabelle said, nestling into him. "So am I."

# About Mary Lancaster

Mary Lancaster lives in Scotland with her husband, three mostly grown-up kids and a small, crazy dog.

Her first literary love was historical fiction, a genre which she relishes mixing up with romance and adventure in her own writing. Her most recent books are light, fun Regency romances written for Dragonblade Publishing: *The Imperial Season* series set at the Congress of Vienna; and the popular*Blackhaven Brides* series, which is set in a fashionable English spa town frequented by the great and the bad of Regency society.

Connect with Mary on-line – she loves to hear from readers:

Email Mary:
Mary@MaryLancaster.com

Website:
www.MaryLancaster.com

Newsletter sign-up:
http://eepurl.com/b4Xoif

Facebook:
facebook.com/mary.lancaster.1656

Facebook Author Page:
facebook.com/MaryLancasterNovelist

Twitter:
@MaryLancNovels

Amazon Author Page:
amazon.com/Mary-Lancaster/e/B00DJ5IACI

Bookbub:
bookbub.com/profile/mary-lancaster

Printed in Great Britain
by Amazon

61890053R00131